A THISTLE & HIVE
CHRISTMAS

ALSO BY JENNAE VALE

THE THISTLE & HIVE SERIES

A Bridge Through Time - Book 1

A Thistle Beyond Time - Book 2

Separated by Time - Book 3

A Matter of Time - Book 4

THE MACKALLS OF DUNNET HEAD

Her Trusted Highlander - Book 1

A HIGHLANDER IN VEGAS

A THISTLE & HIVE CHRISTMAS

A THISTLE & HIVE NOVELLA - BOOK 4.5

JENNAE VALE

For my readers. Without you this wouldn't be possible.

CHAPTER 1

S NOW BLANKETED THE ground and the wind, which had previously been gusting, stilled. Four foot drifts decorated the wooded grove bordering the path as the fanciful red sleigh, led by two enormous horses, glided along on gilded runners. The sleigh was guided by magick, as Beira, the Queen of Winter, covered in fur throws regally lounged on its soft, velvety cushions. The only sounds were the jingling of bells worn by the horses as they jogged along the frozen ground and the soft, sweet song coming from Beira's lips.

Edna Campbell had employed her dear friend to help send word to the MacKenzies, inviting them to come to The Thistle and Hive Inn for a Christmas celebration. Delivering invitations wasn't something that Beira usually did. As a matter of fact, this was a first, but she was happy to help Edna in any way that she could.

The first stop on her journey was the castle of Ewan and Lena MacKenzie. Edna's daughter and son-in-law, along with their two red-headed whirlwinds, Rowan and Ranald, were waiting at the large wooden doors leading into the warmth of their home. The boys excitedly jumped up and down, escaping their mother's grip to run towards the sleigh.

"Rowan! Ranald! Careful, please. Wait for the sleigh to stop," Lena shouted.

"Aye, Ma. We will." Doing as their mother requested, the boys stopped and waited while the sleigh glided to a halt in front of them. Beira stepped lightly from the rig offering a delicate, slender hand to each boy. They eagerly held on, upturned faces filled with

1

awe at the presence of this beautifully ethereal being who seemed to glow as she smiled down at them.

Without saying a word and with only a nod of her head, Beira led the two boys back to their parents. Once there, she reached into her leather satchel and removed a golden envelope, which she handed to Lena. The boys were quieter than they'd ever been, staring with amazement from the faerie queen to the envelope. Beira once again reached into her satchel, removing two special candy treats - one for each boy.

"What do ye say?" Lena asked.

"Thank ye!" they both spoke as one.

Lena opened the envelope as Ewan peered over her shoulder.

You are cordially invited to
Christmas
at
The Thistle & Hive
please be at the bridge by sunrise on
December 22
where you will be guided across by
your hostess, Edna Campbell

"Are we to RSVP to ye..." Lena began to ask, but not knowing the faerie's name she only gazed into her lovely face and waited.

"Beira," the faerie queen supplied. "Yes, I will give Edna yer answer."

"Then tell her we would be delighted to spend the holiday with her and my Da." Lena smiled warmly at Beira, who dropped into a dainty curtsey.

"She will be happy to hear it, and now I must go. I have more invitations to deliver." Beira was snuggled comfortably into the sleigh in the blink of an eye.

The family waved goodbye until the sleigh was out of sight.

Beira was next off to Breaghacraig. How she would get there all in the same day was her own little secret, but as the horses trotted along at a seemingly normal pace, the scenery she passed was a blur. Occasionally she would stop to spend a moment with her forest friends who all greeted her with love in their hearts. The wolf, the fox, the stags and does, along with the smaller creatures, rabbits, squirrels and birds waited by the side of the road for her to arrive. She acknowledged them all with a pat on the head or a scratch behind the ears, a special treat for each and a few moments of her time. These woodland creatures were dear to her heart and it showed.

Soon, as she left the shelter of the trees, Beira saw Breaghacraig. Her magick slowed the horses to a more normal trot as she passed the small crofts that dotted the landscape on the approach to the beautifully imposing castle situated on the other side of the valley. Men, women and children came out to wave as she passed. Some didn't dare leave their cottages, but instead peeked through their window or a crack in their door. She smiled beatifically at them all and returned their waves. In her wake she left small gifts of food and warm clothing for each. Reaching the end of the crofts, Beira noted that a tiny village was cropping up near the gates of the castle and the centerpiece was an inn obviously modeled after Edna's Thistle and Hive. She smiled to herself, knowing that Edna would be most pleased to hear this.

The gates of the castle flew open as she approached and as the horses and sleigh passed through, Beira saw that all activity in the bailey had come to a halt as the castle residents gazed with question at the unusual conveyance that had just entered the courtyard. Beira stood and announced to no one in particular, "I'm here for Laird and Lady MacKenzie."

A young lad broke away from the group and headed for the castle doors. "I'll get them fer ye," he said as he entered.

Moments later the door opened and Robert and Irene MacKenzie exited. On seeing them, the faerie queen left the sleigh and met them as they came down the steps into the courtyard.

Once again, she removed a golden envelope from her satchel,

this time handing it to Laird Robert MacKenzie, who opened it and upon reading it smiled broadly at the willowy faerie before handing it to his wife, Irene. She clasped her husband's arm and gazed hopefully into his face.

"Can we go, Robert?" she asked.

"Aye. I believe we shall go," Robert confirmed.

"What's going on?" Cailin approached along with Cormac and their wives, Ashley and Jenna.

"We've been invited to The Thistle and Hive Inn for Christmas."

"Oh, my goodness, really?" Ashley grabbed the invitation from Irene's hand and showed it to Jenna. "We're all invited?" She looked to Beira for her answer.

"Aye. All of ye. The wee one's as well." Happy faces peered back at her. "I'll tell Edna ye've accepted then?"

"Aye. We'll be there," Robert responded.

The children ran up to see what was happening and Beira happily handed each of them their special treat, which they accepted with much gratitude. "I'll be on my way. I have one more stop to make today."

Gazing back, Beira saw that the family stood by and watched her go, first at a normal clip and then swiftly disappearing from their sight.

Once again she employed her magick to move her conveyance quickly and effortlessly, this time to English lands where she was to see Sir Richard Jefford and his lovely wife, Angelina. A special invitation had been sent for Sir Richard's mother, whom Edna was aware wanted to experience the adventure of time travel. If she accepted the invitation to join the others at the bridge on the twenty-second of December, her wish would soon be granted.

Approaching Sir Richard's home, Beira noted riders in the distance. In the blink of an eye she was upon them and slowed so as not to frighten them. The man rode a large black stallion and the two women rode smaller grey palfreys. They came to a halt as she approached and waited for her sleigh to come up alongside.

"Good day to you," the man said. "May I be of assistance."

"I'm here to see Sir Richard Jefford. Do ye ken where I may find him?" Beira tipped her head, examining the man.

"You can find him here. I'm Sir Richard," he responded.

Beira's happiness shined on her face. "I have something fer ye and fer yer mother." Beira reached into her satchel to extract two invitations, which she handed to Sir Richard. He in turn handed one to the older woman riding with him. Beira assumed this to be his mother.

"What is it?" the younger woman asked.

"It's an invitation to spend Christmas at The Thistle and Hive in Glendaloch." Richard held the invitation in his hand and continued reading.

"An invitation to the future?" the older woman asked.

"Yes, mother. An invitation to the future. Would you like to go?"

"Oh, I would. More than anything."

"Then we shall." Richard gazed at Beira, who nodded her understanding.

"I will let Edna know to expect ye. 'Tis important that ye be at the bridge on the day and at the time Edna has requested."

"Would you care to join us for our evening meal?" Richard's mother asked. "We're heading back that way now."

"I'm afraid I must be on my way. I've much to do. There's never a moment of rest for the Queen of Winter, ye ken." With a wave of her hand, Beira set off in her sleigh. Gazing up at the sky she noted its whiteness and, with some softly whispered words, snowflakes gently began to fall all around her. Pleased with herself, she headed for home and the sweetness it would bring her, as soon as she delivered the exciting news to her friend.

CHAPTER 2

T O SAY SHE was excited, would be putting it mildly. Edna Campbell, the witch who guarded the bridge through time, was doing something she'd never done before. She was welcoming several of her time travel veterans and their families to join her at The Thistle and Hive Inn for the Christmas holiday. She couldn't think of anything that would make her happier than to share *this* experience with *this* particular group of travelers.

Edna had requested that they be at the bridge by sunrise and as the first glimmers of sunlight were making their appearance in the sky, her guests were all waiting there as requested, with the exception of Sir Richard and his group. She would wait for them to appear before conjuring the fog that would bring them all the way from the sixteenth century to the twenty-first. She could see the others talking and laughing while they waited. Some of them had never made the journey before and she could sense their nervousness. She could see them all, but they had no idea she watched them.

"Is anyone else joining us?" Ashley asked.

The others shrugged their shoulders at this question. The children were getting fidgety. It had been a long trip for them and they were excited to cross the bridge. Cailin held tightly to baby Emma, who was swaddled in furs and the warmth of her father's arms. She was such a tiny little thing and she appeared to be even tinier being held in the arms of this braw highlander. Edna chuckled to herself. She could hardly wait to hold the babe in her arms and to hug all the other little ones, but especially her own two grandsons, Ranald and Rowan.

At the sound of approaching horses, all heads turned to see who was arriving. Edna breathed a sigh of relief as Sir Richard, Angelina and Richard's mother, Lady Catherine, approached the others. Angelina had her new son, Henry, swaddled in a cloth sling that his mother had obviously fashioned for him. Happy shouts greeted Richard and were returned in kind.

"Richard! Yer joining us!" Robert rode to his side and shook his hand.

"Angelina, you have a baby!" Ashley exclaimed, almost coming out of her seat to get a peek.

"I do. His name is Henry and he's the handsomest little lad you'll ever see." Angelina replied. "When we get to the inn you'll see for yourself."

"How old is he?" Ashley asked.

"Three months. Is Cailin holding your little bundle of joy?"

"Aye. I am. Our little Emma." Cailin replied.

"This is going to be so much fun," Angelina gushed. "I can hardly wait to exchange baby stories with you, Ashley."

Edna noticed that Jenna, who had seemed excited to see everyone only moments before, didn't participate in this conversation at all and instead turned her horse to face away from the others and towards the bridge. Edna wasn't sure what the problem was, but she'd find out soon enough.

Once everyone enough time to get their greetings out of the way, she called upon the fog to descend on the bridge. Those who were waiting stopped talking to silently watch the fog as it swirled at the edge of the bridge. Cailin took the lead, having made this journey before. He was followed by Cormac and the others. Two by two they made their way into the fog, where colorful lights popped and sparked, following them until they had safely crossed the bridge where Edna waited beaming with joy.

"Welcome!" Edna shouted.

"Edna!" The others cried on seeing her. Behind them the fog stopped swirling and gradually dissipated.

Edna found herself surrounded by her guests as they dismounted and each hugged and kissed her in turn. "I'm so excited to see ye all." Edna wiped the happy tears, which had formed, from her eyes. "Follow me. Angus and Teddy are waiting for us at the inn."

Ranald and Rowan each took one of her hands as she led the way along the path that led to the main street of Glendaloch. The group following her were a mix of amazed at what they were seeing and happy to be back.

"Thank ye so much for inviting us," Robert said as he rode up beside Edna and the children. They were all following her as if she were the Pied Piper.

"'Tis my pleasure to have ye all here with me," Edna answered. "Are ye excited to be here, Robert?"

"Aye. We all are. Irene and the children havenae ceased speaking of it since we received yer invitation. 'Tis the journey of a lifetime fer me family."

Reaching the roadway, they rounded the corner and paraded down the center of the street. The people of Glendaloch waved happily at the group as they passed. Over the years, they had seen many things which had become commonplace to them, not the least of which was the costumed Highlanders Edna brought to town every so often.

The street was decorated with garland and ribbons and later when the sun set, colorful fairy lights would turn the small town into a magical wonderland. As they approached the inn, Angus and Teddy stood waiting with huge grins on their faces.

"This is it," Edna said. "The Thistle and Hive Inn. Angus will lead the men down to the stables, where there are warm stalls and feed for the horses."

The women dismounted and Cailin handed Emma down to Ashley who cradled her protectively in her arms.

"I must get a peek at this wee one." Edna placed an arm around Ashley as she cooed to Emma and touched her cheek. "Arenae ye a wee beauty? Ye look just like yer mother." Emma took Edna's finger in her tiny hand and held tightly. "And with the strength of yer father."

"Thank you, Edna. Without your meddling, there wouldn't be a little Emma," Ashley teased.

"I'm a meddler, yer right, but always with good reason." Edna's face lit up as Emma cooed and her tiny rosebud lips broke into a big smile. "Oh. I dinnae think I can stand it another moment. May I?" She put her arms out to hold Emma.

"Of course," Ashley handed Emma over to her and the baby gazed at Edna in fascination.

The others were all chatting excitedly, ogling and pointing at every unusual thing in their line of vision.

"Shall we take the horses, then?" Angus asked. He climbed atop Ashley's horse and Teddy took the reins of Lady Catherine's mount. The men all ponied their wives horses and headed off up the street to the stable at the far end of town. "We'll be back shortly," Angus said to the women. Wee Robert took charge of his own mount and after his sisters dismounted, ponied the horse that had held his siblings.

"Shall we go in?" Edna asked. "Let's get ye all warm by the fire and then I'll show ye to yer rooms."

As the doors to the inn opened, the smiling faces of Maggie and Dylan, accompanied by a wriggling Chester, greeted them.

"Welcome! Come in!" Maggie made a welcoming gesture with her arm and Dylan did the same, guiding the travelers into the cozy lobby of the inn.

Edna, still holding Emma, led the way into the dining room where there were plates of freshly baked scones and mugs of warm cider for the adults, and cupcakes and hot chocolate for the children.

"Dylan, I'm so excited to see you. I've missed you so much," Jenna said through happy tears as she made her way into her cousin's embrace.

"I've missed you, too." He gently kissed the top of her head and then held her away from himself, as if he needed to be sure it was really Jenna.

THE CHILDREN MADE a beeline for the treats and Maggie helped them with plates and napkins. She got them all seated while their parents chatted with Edna and Dylan. Chester wandered from person to person, greeting each before moving on. He finally settled on the floor by the children, obviously hoping they'd share their cupcakes with him.

"What do ye think?" Maggie asked. "Do ye like the cupcakes?"

"Aye. They be verra good. What is this drink?" Fiona asked as she took another sip.

"'Tis hot chocolate. I ken ye've never had it, but isnae it delicious?"

"Mmmm…" was the response. Fiona gazed up at Maggie and all the other children giggled at the dollop of whipped cream that had somehow made its way onto the tip of Fiona's nose. Maggie gently wiped it away with a napkin and Fiona smiled brightly at her, before taking another cookie. "Everything is so pretty," Fiona said as she looked around the room.

Edna and Maggie had decorated it with the children in mind. The tree was enormous, practically touching the ceiling and it was covered with many colorful ornaments and sparkling lights. A giant star adorned the very top. The windows and doors were framed by garland and more lights, and a candle sat on each sill.

It wasn't long before Ranald and Rowan began racing around the room and peeking their heads into every doorway.

"Ranald! Rowan! Settle down. Yer Grannie doesnae wish ye to tear apart her home in the first few moments yer here." Lena broke away from the adults and brought the two young lads back to their seats. "Ye must behave yerselves. Ye can play once we've all gotten settled. Do ye ken my meaning?"

"Aye." Rowan smiled sweetly at his mother.

"Ranald?" Lena asked.

"Aye." He seemed somewhat reluctant to concede, but when

Lena leaned down and kissed his cheek, he said, "I'll be good, Ma."

Maggie exchanged a knowing glance with Lena. "I've got it from here."

"Ashley, Jenna, ye and yer husbands and baby Emma will stay in the cottage behind the inn. There is plenty of room for all of ye and ye'll have some privacy. I'll show ye the way once the men are back from the stables."

"Thank you, Edna. It sounds wonderful." Jenna said.

"Lena, ye and Ewan will have yer old bedroom and the little ones will all be sharing a room. Irene, Angelina and Catherine, ye'll all have rooms upstairs, but first help yerselves to the scones and a nice warm drink, please."

"I can hardly wait." Ashley broke away from the group and headed straight to the refreshments and the hot chocolate. "Mmmm…" She took a sip of the chocolate. "I love chocolate so much. How I've missed you." She spoke directly to the cup and the others all chuckled as they tried the scones, which much to Edna's delight seemed to be a huge success. Everyone took a seat at the table next to the children. The cozy warmth of the inn was something that Edna prided herself on and she was happy to see how at home her guests felt since their arrival.

The doors to the inn opened and the men along with wee Robert entered and joined their wives in the dining room, taking seats at another nearby table. Cormac was greeted by a bounding Chester, who practically leaped into his arms.

"I see ye've missed me as much as I've missed ye." Cormac hugged an obviously ecstatic Chester, who rolled over for a belly scratch.

Edna brought the baked goods to the men, along with mugs. "I've coffee if ye'd rather that." Edna said.

"Aye. I'd like that," Cailin said with a gleam in his eye.

"Cormac?"

"Aye," he replied.

"I'll have some as well," Richard said.

"Robert, I ken that neither of these drinks is familiar to ye, but what would ye care to try?"

He glanced at the other men and decided, "Coffee."

"Alright then, coffee all around."

"I'll help ye, me love," Angus offered, following her into the kitchen.

She peeked back over her shoulder to make sure everyone was happy and seeing that they were, closed the door behind her. "Angus, this is going to be a verra happy time for all, dinnae ye think so?"

"Aye. So far all is well. No one seems too shocked to be here," he chuckled.

"I can hardly believe they're all here. I've been looking forward to this for months with all the planning and preparation."

"I'm just happy they accepted the invitation." Angus winked at Edna.

"Oh, come here ye silly man."

Angus obliged his wife and she rewarded him with a kiss which, she noted, he took full advantage of.

CHAPTER 3

ASHLEY, CAILIN, JENNA & CORMAC

T HE LOVELY LITTLE cottage behind the inn was exactly what Ashley had expected. As they walked through the arched wooden doorway, they entered a sitting room with a comfy sofa and loveseat, all set around the hearth of an old stone fireplace. A small kitchen off to the right would be perfect for their needs, with a small stove and refrigerator.

Jenna and Cormac were exploring the two bedrooms. "This one must be for you two. There's a cradle in there for Emma," Jenna noted.

"Perfect," Ashley remarked. She handed Emma to Cailin and headed for the bedroom. "This is so pretty. What do you think, Cailin?"

"I think 'tis a lovely place to spend time with ye and our wee lass." Cailin placed a sleeping Emma into the cradle and returned to Ashley's side where they both admired their beautiful daughter. "I can hardly believe we're back here in Glendaloch, married and with a wee bairn of our own."

"All thanks to Edna." Ashley wrapped her arms around Cailin's waist and he pulled her close. Resting her head on his chest, she could hear the familiar sound of his heart beating a calm tattoo, and in the warmth of his embrace she relaxed as she always did. He was her rock. The man she loved more than she could ever express. She hoped he knew just how important he was to her. She simply couldn't imagine a life without him in it.

"What are ye thinking, lass?" Cailin asked.

Ashley tipped her head back, looked up into his soft grey eyes and smiled. "Nothing. Just enjoying my hug."

"Yer hugging me so tight, I'm afraid ye may break me," he teased.

"I don't think I could do that even if I tried," she giggled. "Let's go enjoy that comfy sofa and the fireplace. We'll let Emma sleep for a while."

They both took another look at a sleeping Emma before retreating from the room to find that Cormac and Jenna had closeted themselves in their bedroom. Cailin glanced from the closed door to Ashley and winked. "Shall we?" he pointed to the sofa.

He sprawled across the sofa and Ashley joined him, snuggling into his arms. Her life really had turned out to be happier than she'd ever thought it could be back in San Francisco. The only thing she worried about was Emma.

"Cailin, while we're here, I'd like Emma to see Dr. Ferguson. You know, to make sure she's okay and we have nothing to worry about."

"Whatever ye like, love. I dinnae believe he'll find any problems."

"I know. It's just that she's so precious, I don't want anything to happen to her." This was a conversation she'd had with him many times. She worried about Emma getting sick and not having access to modern medicine. Many children didn't make it to adulthood in the sixteenth century and she wanted to be sure that Emma wasn't going to be one of them.

"Ashley, if it makes ye feel better ye should do it. I have nae objections."

EVER SINCE EMMA'S birth, Cailin had noticed a change in Ashley. She worried constantly about Emma being ill. So far they hadn't experienced anything more than a slight cold. As a matter of fact, Cailin had marveled at just how healthy his little daughter was. Ashley had panicked at the onset of the cold and would listen to no one, not even Irene who was raising four children of her own.

During the brief course of the illness, Ashley had been inconsolable, hovering over Emma constantly, to the point where she hardly ate or slept for fear that something would happen if she took a few moments away from the baby to care for herself. He would definitely have to speak with Edna to see what they could do to put Ashley's fears to rest. Seeing Dr. Ferguson would help in the short term, but he wanted to have a plan in place if need be.

"I love you, Cailin," Ashley gazed up at him, trust in her amber eyes. "So, so much."

"And I love ye. While we're here ye've nothing to fear, so I want ye to enjoy yerself. Dinnae think about the things that worry ye."

"I'll try," she said. "I'm tired. I think I'll take a little nap." Ashley made herself comfortable in his arms and closed her eyes.

Looking down at Ashley's sleeping face, Cailin couldn't help but remember their first meeting, when he had unknowingly crossed the bridge through time to rescue Ashley from poor Teddy. When he'd thrown Teddy over the bridge and into the water, Cailin had no idea that Teddy was inadvertently part of Edna's plan to get the two of them together. Teddy had forgiven him though and he'd ended up the luckiest of men to have found Ashley and made her his. He'd do anything for her. He only wanted her to be happy and to feel safe and secure.

"How AMAZING is this?" Jenna twirled around the room enjoying the comfy warmth of the bedroom she'd share with her handsome husband.

"Are ye happy to be back in yer own time, Jenna?" Cormac seemed worried.

"Of course I'm happy, but don't worry I'm going home with you when our visit is over." She stopped in front of Cormac and poked him in the ribs. "What about you? Are you happy to be here?"

"Aye. 'Tis good to be away from the castle for a while. I'm grateful to Edna for inviting us."

"It's just what we needed… a nice little vacation." Jenna had been stressed out about the fact that she couldn't get pregnant, no matter how much they tried. Everywhere she looked she saw pregnant women. She couldn't seem to get away from them. Her dear friend Ashley had just confided to her that she thought she might be pregnant *again* and while Jenna was happy for her, she couldn't help but feel disappointed at her own predicament. Even Aunt Angelina had a baby. Jenna was shocked and though she hated to admit it, a bit jealous too. She had almost lost it back at the bridge. The urge to cry over her inability to conceive was so strong that she couldn't even look at Ashley and Angelina. The number of women she knew who had and were having babies was growing along with her fear that she would never have the pleasure of holding her own child.

Cormac seemed to be reading her mind as he stood with his head cocked to the side, and a knowing look on his face. "Jenna, dinnae fear. We have all the time in the world to have a babe."

"But what if we don't?" Jenna's eyes began to tear up. She knew how much Cormac wanted a child of his own. He loved baby Emma and his other nieces and nephews, but he'd told her more than once how happy he'd be when it was his turn to be a father.

Cormac pulled her in for a hug. Kissing the top of her head. "If we don't, I'll still love ye just as much as I do now," he reassured her. "Though we'll surely keep trying, as I enjoy that part verra, verra much."

Jenna couldn't help but laugh. Cormac was the most relaxed, fun man she'd ever known. Nothing seemed to bother him and while she'd been a bit of a bitch when they'd first met, as well as her own worst enemy, he'd been the bright light at the end of the tunnel that had grown brighter every day she'd known him. She wanted to be a mother, but more than anything she wanted him to have his wish to be a father.

"Are ye happy to see yer cousin Dylan?" It was obvious Cormac wanted to change the topic.

"Yes. I've really missed him. And I've missed Chester, too."

"Chester was me best companion when he lived at Breaghacraig." Cormac's face broke into a grin and Jenna's did as well.

"Dylan always said that dog loved you more than him," she pointed out.

"I dinnae believe that. He was happy to leave with Dylan." Cormac sat on the edge of the bed with a thoughtful expression on his face. "But then again, no one asked him if he'd rather stay with me." He lay back on the pillows with his arms behind his head and chuckled.

Jenna sat on the bed next to him and had to laugh. No matter what her mood, Cormac could always bring a smile to her lips and make her laugh. She really did love that about him.

"Now. I'm feeling the need to try to make a baby again. Are ye with me?" Cormac pulled Jenna down next to him.

Jenna gazed lovingly into his eyes. "Yes. Let's do it." She leaned over him and kissed him, showing him all the love she felt in her heart, determined today would be the day both of their dreams would come true.

CHAPTER 4

LENA & EWAN

"LENA CAMPBELL? Is it really ye?" A tall thin man dressed in the strange manner of these future people, stopped them as they were about to pass.

Ewan placed a protective arm around his wife and glowered at the man standing in front of them. Lena, for her part, seemed at a loss for words. Ewan knew the people of Glendaloch hadn't seen her for years and her mysterious disappearance and reappearance had tongues wagging all over the sleepy little village. It was especially difficult for his wife to explain what had happened and it seemed this was one of those moments.

"It's me, Michael." He paused, waiting for an answer. "Ye don't remember me, do ye?"

"Michael." Lena whispered his name.

"Yes. It's me! I heard ye were back. How've ye been?"

Ewan spoke up. "What is it ye want with me wife?" He rose to his full height and made himself as menacing as possible.

The man didn't seem to notice, standing there smiling like a giddy fool and gawking at Lena as if he'd never seen a woman before.

"I'm sorry, I should have introduced myself. I'm Michael Allaway, Lena's…" He stopped short of finishing his sentence and glanced Lena's way, his brow furrowed in obvious concern.

"It's alright, Ewan. Ye can relax. Michael is an old friend." Much to Ewan's surprise, she shrugged out of his embrace and hugged this old friend, even kissing his cheek.

Ewan harrumphed, letting his displeasure show. He didn't believe he could possibly scowl or stare daggers at the man any more than he already had. His wife was gazing at the fool with warmth in her eyes and, were those unshed tears he saw about to spill from those emerald green pools. The "old" friend as Lena had identified him was now holding her hands.

"I thought I'd never see ye again," he said, "and yet here ye stand."

If this besotted idjit didn't stop staring at and touching his wife, Ewan was afraid he may have to resort to violence. Lena was *his* woman, *his* wife. How dare this man flirt with her before his very eyes.

"I'm sorry. I didn't mean to frighten everyone." Lena smiled sweetly and Ewan narrowed his eyes, prepared to do battle if necessary.

He'd seen her smile at many, after all it was her nature to be kind and caring, but this unsettled him. Something about their behavior told him there was much more here than met the eye.

"How long are ye here for?" Michael asked.

"We leave the day after Christmas."

"If ye can get away, maybe we can get together and reminisce about old times."

"I'd like that very much." Lena's face brightened and Ewan's heart sank.

"I'll be in touch then." He leaned in to kiss her cheek, lingering just a bit longer than necessary, Ewan controlled the urge to come between them as Michael took a moment to inhale Lena's scent.

"It was a pleasure meeting ye, Ewan." Michael waved as he turned and walked away.

Ewan snarled a response and Lena watched Michael as he slowly receded from view.

Silence descended on the pair and lingered before Ewan finally spoke, doing his best to control his anger and jealousy. He softened his voice. "If I'm nae mistaken, that man was more than an old friend to ye. Do ye care to tell me who he really is?"

Lena's sad smile spoke volumes, but she said, "Just someone I knew a long time ago." Taking Ewan's hand, she led him away down the street.

CHANCES OF RUNNING into people from her past were pretty much one hundred percent here in Glendaloch. The entire village new exactly who she was and while they were all curious about where she'd spent the last several years of her life, they'd all behaved as if she'd only been off on a long vacation. The one person she'd both wanted to see and hoped not to see was Michael Allaway. At one point, in her teenage years, she thought they'd marry and raise a family here in Glendaloch, but then her curiosity got the better of her and she'd crossed the bridge, met Ewan and never looked back. She knew she should tell Ewan, but she didn't wish to upset him. Lena snuggled up close and felt him relax. It was best to leave the past in the past.

Ewan was staring at her as they walked. "Are ye well, Lena?"

"Aye. 'Tis strange being back here after so many years." She glanced down the street and shook her head. "'Tis still the same. It looks the same as it did the day I left."

"Are ye sorry ye left?" Ewan appeared apprehensive of what she might say.

"Of course not. If I hadn't left, I would never have met ye and I wouldn't have our two little red-headed imps. I love our home. I'm happy to be here and to see Ma and Da, but I'll be just as happy to leave with ye and the boys."

"Are ye sure?" He obviously needed reassurance, which was a most unusual thing for Ewan.

"Verra sure." Lena turned to face him, stroking his face and noting how very handsome he was. She stood on tiptoe and kissed his lips, eliciting a soft growl from him as his arms tightened around her waist and he prolonged the kiss.

It was odd to see Ewan in this light. Ever since the day she'd met him, he'd been so very sure of himself when it came to her. He had a strong, commanding presence, which was tempered with a softness reserved only for her and the boys. She didn't want him to doubt her love for him for even a moment. Perhaps coming back to Glendaloch had been a terrible mistake, but they were here now and she'd have to make the best of a very odd situation. She did want to see Michael. She had to explain to him what had happened, even if he didn't understand it. On the other hand, she knew Ewan wouldn't be happy about that, but she had to have some closure with Michael, if not for herself, then for him.

"You two should get a room," Dylan's voice laughingly called from across the street. He waved at them and then took Maggie by the hand and crossed the street.

"Hi," Maggie said. "Are ye having fun exploring?"

"Aye. We are," Ewan stated. "Lena has been showing me all the places she has told me about. She has painted the perfect picture. If I were to come upon it on my own, I'd know it was Glendaloch."

"Well, I'm happy yer enjoying it. Dylan and I were just going to stop into the pub for some lunch, would ye like to join us?"

"Are ye nae cooking lunch at the inn?" Lena asked Dylan.

"Not today. You, Ewan, Irene and Robert are out exploring and the others are all in their rooms resting from the trip here. I know everyone enjoyed the snacks when they arrived, so I left some sandwiches and fruit for them if they're hungry when they come out of their rooms. I wanted to take my lady out and we'd love it if you'd join us. It'd give us some time to get better acquainted."

"Please join us," Maggie added.

"What would ye like to do, Lena?" Ewan asked.

"I'd like to have lunch with my cousin and her man," Lena answered.

Ewan nodded his agreement.

"Shall we then?" Dylan led the way with Maggie by his side.

They entered Calhoun's Pub and took a seat in the first booth they came to.

"Four pints please, Daniel, and four orders of fish and chips."

"As ye wish, Dylan." Daniel Calhoun, the proprietor's son was behind the bar. He called the order to his father in the back. "Da, four fish and chips."

"I hope that's alright with ye," Maggie said. "If ye'd rather, we can get some menus and ye can choose yer own lunch."

"Fish and chips will be wonderful," Lena said. "When I lived here, they were always the best." She gazed at Ewan who appeared quite at home sitting next to her. "Yer going to love it, Ewan."

"What are chips?" he asked.

"Ye'll see. It's too difficult to explain."

Ewan seemed satisfied with that answer and settled in to a question and answer period with Dylan, asking him about everything unrecognizable that he'd come across.

Daniel delivered the pints to the table. "Here ye are."

"Thanks, Daniel," Dylan said.

"Lena Campbell, is that ye?" He examined her face for a moment. "Of course 'tis. I'd recognize ye anywhere. How've ye been."

"Fine, Daniel and yerself?" She caught a glimpse of Ewan out of the corner of her eye and noted that he seemed uncomfortable once again.

"Good. I'm still here in Glendaloch, working for my Da as ye can plainly see."

In an effort to put Ewan at ease, she introduced Daniel. "Ewan, this is Daniel Calhoun. His sister and I were the very best of friends."

"As the baby brother, it was my duty to make their lives as miserable as possible. I think I did a fairly good job, wouldnae ye say, Lena."

"Aye. Ye did. There were many times when yer sister and I plotted to lock ye in the basement just so ye'd leave us alone."

Daniel had developed a deep belly laugh, which caused Lena and the others to join him. He was all grown up now and no longer the pesky little brother she'd once known.

"How is Mary?" Lena asked. She hadn't seen her old friend since just before she made the crossing.

"Mary's fine. She's living in London now with her artist boyfriend."

He put finger quotes around the word artist.

"Is she really? I never thought she'd be the one to leave Glendaloch and I assumed ye wouldnae be able to wait to get out of here."

"I thought the same," said Daniel, "but as ye can see I'm firmly ensconced here in town."

"Are ye married?"

"Nay. I'm waiting fer the right woman to make her way into town. So far, no luck." Again he chuckled. "Maybe yer mother will do some of her matchmaking magick for me."

"Ye never know, she just might."

"Daniel, pick up yer order!" Mr. Calhoun shouted through the kitchen pass through.

"Aye, Da. Ye'll never guess who's here."

"I don't suppose ye could just tell me. I hate these guessing games." Mr. Calhoun seemed his old impatient self.

"Lena Campbell, Mary's friend."

The door to the kitchen flew open and Mr. Calhoun strode quickly to their table, lifting Lena from her seat and hugging her so tightly she thought her eyes were being squeezed from her head. Next he held her away from him and tipped his head from side to side examining her face. "Aye. 'Tis ye." He pulled her back in for another hug.

"Mr. Calhoun, I cannae breathe," Lena gasped.

"I'm sorry, Lena. I never thought to see ye here in town again. Our Mary missed ye so after ye left, as did the missus and I."

"I spent a lot of time here with all of ye," Lena smiled fondly at father and son. "This is my husband, Ewan."

Ewan stood and extended a hand to first father and then son. "I'm pleased to make yer acquaintance, sir."

"As are we," Daniel said.

"We're back visiting Ma for the holiday with our two sons and some other members of Ewan's family. I hope ye'll stop by for our Christmas Eve celebration."

"We just might do that, lass. I'm closing the pub early to be sure everyone is home with their families, as they should be on a night like that."

"Good. I'll tell Ma and Da to expect ye then." Lena sat back down. "I can hardly wait to taste yer famous fish and chips."

Mr. Calhoun looked back to the pass through, jumping into action as he retrieved the food and brought it to them. "Here ye are. Lunch is on me today and I'll nae hear another word about it."

"Thank you so much, Mr. Calhoun. We appreciate it," Dylan said. "Would you care to join us?"

"Nae. I'll let ye enjoy the food and I'll see ye on Christmas Eve. I can hardly wait to meet yer little ones, lass." With that he turned and went back into the kitchen and Daniel retreated to the bar.

Ewan squeezed her hand under the table. "Ye've many good friends here in Glendaloch."

"Aye. I do."

THE WALK BACK to the inn was a quiet one. They were all quite stuffed from their meal.

"I hope the boys are napping," Lena said. "I think I'd like to do the same."

"Dylan and I will watch them so ye can have a rest," Maggie volunteered.

"That's so sweet of ye both. Thank ye."

They opened the door to the inn and were greeted by Edna and Angus. "Did ye have fun, Ewan?" was the first question out of Edna's mouth.

"I did." Ewan gazed at Lena who was yawning and leaning into him. "We're verra tired though. We thought we'd take a bit of a rest."

"Oh, please do. Lena before ye go, Michael Allaway called. He wanted to know if he could take ye to lunch tomorrow."

Ewan did his best to control his jealousy. This was merely an old friend and he trusted Lena to have lunch with him without incident, but why did he feel there was something more to it. She looked to him and he nodded.

"What did ye tell him, Ma?"

"I said ye'd be happy to."

"Ewan do ye want to join us?" Lena appeared worried.

"Nae, love. Ye go and enjoy yer time with yer friend."

"Are ye sure?"

"Aye. Dinnae worry about me." *I'll be busy worrying about ye, my love.*

CHAPTER 5

"Ooo, Robert, I love it here. Do we have to go back?" Irene was mesmerized by all the unusual things she was seeing at the local apothecary. She picked up everything that caught her eye and examined it from top to bottom. "I'll have much to ask Edna when we return to the inn."

Robert smiled adoringly at his wife. "Irene, no matter how much ye love it, we must go back to Breaghacraig when the time arrives." It was their first afternoon in Glendaloch and they were both excited to explore, so they'd left the children with Edna and headed out. For his part, Robert also spent a lot of time pushing buttons, pulling levers and generally trying to figure out how all these modern luxuries worked. He'd already decided he wanted a shower, although he had absolutely no idea at all how to create one. Plumbing is what Angus had called it, trying his best to explain the workings to a puzzled Robert.

He finally managed to pull Irene away from the apothecary and their next stop was the hardware store. His eyes lit when he saw things that he recognized as parts to the light fixtures. "Mayhap I'll find what I need here in this store." Robert took off and left Irene running to keep up with him.

"Robert! Wait!" she called after him.

"Dinnae fear my sweet, I'll nae leave ye. Come. I think I see things to make a shower."

"Robert, ye cannae possibly believe ye'll make one."

"Do ye doubt me, Irene?"

"Nae," she admitted. "I ken when ye decide to do something that ye'll move heaven and earth to do it." As they walked, Robert stopped at a wall of books. "Irene. Can ye believe it. Do ye see all the books?"

"Aye, Robert. I do."

He searched each title and then exclaimed, "Here. 'Tis a book I can use." Robert happily grabbed the book and held on tightly, a huge grin on his handsome face. "Look Irene, it says, 'Plumbing.' 'Tis what Angus called the workings of the shower."

"Can ye nae make a room without a roof?" Irene tipped her head in question.

"Nae roof?" Robert was puzzled by her question.

"Aye. Then when it rains ye can stand in it and 'twill be like yer fancy shower that ye love so much." Irene giggled and Robert knew she was teasing him.

He broke into laughter so loud that others in the store turned to look at them. "Come let's purchase this book."

Robert continued walking, searching for someone to help him buy the book. Eventually he saw a man wearing an apron, who looked as good as anyone to speak with.

"Sir. I wish to purchase this book."

"Aye. I can help ye," the man answered.

"Edna Campbell requested that ye put it on her bill."

"If ye'll come with me, I'll take care of it." He reached for the book, but Robert wasn't about to let it leave his grasp. The man shook his head and gave Robert an odd look, but turned and walked away. "Follow me."

He led them to the front of the store where he stood behind a counter and punched buttons on some strange contraption that Robert found fascinating. The man reached a hand out for the book and again Robert held onto it tightly. "Sir, I need the book so I can ring it up for ye."

"I don't understand," Robert said.

Irene elbowed him in the side and nodded her head in the man's direction. Robert reluctantly handed the book over and the man passed some strange wand over it before handing it right back to Robert. "Here ye go. This will appear on Mrs. Campbell's bill. Ye must be one of her out of town guests," the man observed.

"We are indeed," Robert responded.

"Well, enjoy yer stay. If ye need anything else, please come back and see us."

"I may be back. I wish to build a shower."

"We have everything ye'd need for that, sir."

"Good." Robert took Irene's hand and tucked it in his as he walked away with his book.

"WHERE SHALL WE go next," Irene asked. She was thoroughly enjoying herself and the company of her husband. "The children are fine with Edna and I've no wish to go back yet."

"I've no idea where to go next, love. Let's just walk." Robert led her down the street where they peered into the store windows as they passed by. It was beginning to get dark and the fairy lights strung up and down the street went on, causing Irene to gasp at their beauty. "Robert, arenae they wonderful. Yet another thing I'd like to bring back to Breaghacraig."

"I'll ask Angus about them. Mayhap they have them at the hardware store." He pulled Irene closer. "Are ye warm enough, Irene?"

"Aye. I'm always warm when ye've yer arm wrapped around me."

He sweetly kissed the top of her head. This is a rare time fer us. 'Tis not often that we are completely alone."

"I'd forgotten what it could be like." Robert was right. The business of running Breaghacraig, caring for their children and Robert's position as Laird of the clan meant their lives were quite busy and filled with children and castle residents who were always in need of something. Before they married, they'd had much more time to themselves and it was nice they'd been given this opportunity to reacquaint themselves with each other. "I'd like to do something nice for Edna and Angus. Ye ken to thank them for all of this."

"Aye, but what?"

"We'll speak with the others about it. Maybe one of them will have an idea."

"Very well then. I believe we should head back to the inn. The shops seem to be closing for the night and our children may well have worn out our hosts."

Robert kept Irene tucked close by his side as they made their way back. Irene could feel how relaxed he was and it made her happy. He had so much responsibility on his shoulders all the time. She was proud of him and proud to be married to the Laird of Clan MacKenzie, but she was also happy to have him to herself, even for this brief time.

Reaching the inn, Robert opened the door for Irene and followed her inside. Their children came running.

"Ma! Da!" Isobel called as she wrapped herself around her father's leg. "Where did ye go?"

"We were exploring Glendaloch," Irene said. "Did ye miss us?"

Isobel looked rather sheepishly up at them and whispered, "No."

Irene and Robert chuckled at this and then led the children back into the lobby area of the inn. Angus was sprawled on the floor with the twins, as they did their best to wrestle him into submission. Edna was seated in a nearby chair with a pile of books on the table adjacent to it.

"We were just reading," she said. "The children have been verra well behaved."

"Can Edna keep reading?" Fiona asked. Little Brian climbed up into Edna's lap and made himself at home.

"We're mid-story, so if ye wish to go upstairs and rest, I'm happy to keep reading." Edna waited for their answer and when she didn't receive one, she said, "Go on then. Have a bit of a rest before dinner. I'll call ye when 'tis time."

"Thank ye, Edna. I don't ken how we'll ever repay ye fer yer kindness."

"Don't worry about that. I'm not doing this for payment, I'm doing it out of love."

Irene was so overwhelmed by Edna's statement that she surprised herself by going to her and giving her a big hug and kiss. "Children, continue to be good for Edna. We'll see ye at dinner."

Robert and Irene headed upstairs to their room. "'Tis odd having nothing to do." Robert said as they topped the stairs.

"I can think of something to do, even if ye cannae," Irene winked at him and swiftly opened the door to their room. Robert was quick to follow.

EDNA CHUCKLED TO herself as she watched Irene and Robert retreat to their room. The children, Wee Robert, Fiona, Isobel and Brian, were a delight and Edna was enjoying the fun of spoiling them. They were such well-behaved little ones for the most part. The description did not, however, extend to her own grandsons. Yes, they were adorable, but the two of them could get into more trouble, more quickly than anyone would have imagined possible. It only took a moment of inattention on her part. Speaking of which, she'd been so focused on Irene and Robert that she'd forgotten all about the twins. It was much too quiet for her liking.

"Rowan! Ranald! Where are ye?" Edna called into the silence. No one answered. She cautiously entered the room, searching every corner as she went. She approached the center of the room and stood a moment, knowing that they had to be there somewhere. A swishing sound came from behind her and before she knew it, she had four little arms wrapped around her, tickling her for all they were worth. Robert and Irene's children joined in and Edna hooted with laughter. "Why ye little rascals!" She squirmed out of their grasp and then turned the tables on them, grabbing the first child she could get her hands on. Ranald squealed with laughter. She let him go and one by one she chased them down until they got the tickling they deserved. "Enough of that now." Edna caught her breath. She wasn't as young as she used to be and as much as she wished to run and play with the children, she knew it was probably not the best idea. "Come. Let's sit for a moment and catch our breath." Edna plopped herself down on the sofa and was immediately surrounded with children all trying their best to be the one's sitting right next to her.

"Edna, what are ye doing?" Angus asked as he entered the room.

"'Tis a good question. I'm apparently wearing myself out in an attempt to wear these children out."

"Leave that to me, my love. Children, get yer cloaks and we'll go out back to spar with my straw man." He put his hands on his hips.

"Grandpa, can I go first?" Rowan asked.

"We'll see, lad. Come, let's go. 'Twill be too dark soon."

The children jumped from the sofa and all ran to the coat rack to grab their cloaks. Robert, being the tallest, handed them down to the others.

Edna gazed gratefully at her husband. "Thank ye, Angus. Yer too good to me."

"I won't be long. They'll be ready for their supper and then bed soon enough."

"I'll see to the food, while yer out with them." She watched the little ones all line up behind Angus and head for the door leading to the back. If she wasn't so exhausted she'd go with them, but for now she'd take a quick breather and then head to the kitchen to get their supper together for them.

CHAPTER 6

M AGGIE AND DYLAN were excited to see their old friends, especially Sir Richard. Edna had reassured them that after their battle with Brielle, he was alright, but it was good to see him in the flesh, happy and healthy.

"So yer married," Maggie said.

"I am. And it would seem you are as well." Richard smiled warmly at them both.

Dylan glanced at Maggie, taking her hand and bringing it to his lips. "Happily so."

"We were both so worried about ye. The last time we saw ye the fog was spiriting ye away. We had no idea where ye'd gone off to," Maggie said.

"Edna in her infinite wisdom sent me to San Francisco, where you're from Dylan. I had some lessons to learn about life and love and she knew that. I am a new man because of it." Richard leaned back in his chair appearing relaxed and happy.

"I'm amazed you managed to convince Angelina to marry you. She was always quite the skeptic about love," Dylan said.

"I consider myself lucky to call her wife. She has brought so much to my life, but nothing more precious than my son Henry." Richard's pride showed clearly as his face lit in a huge grin.

"How old is he now?" Maggie asked.

"Three months. Isn't he the handsomest little lad you've ever seen?" Richard was practically gushing as he spoke of his new son. "Fatherhood is wonderful. I highly recommend it, Dylan."

"We're going to wait a while before we have children. We're still young and we've so much we want to do," Dylan responded.

"Are you saying I'm old?" Richard cocked an eyebrow and narrowed his eyes in feigned indignation.

"Of course not. It's just that in your time it was expected that you'd be married and having a family as early as possible. In our time, we'd like to wait until our lives are more settled."

"How much more settled can they be? You seem happy here at the inn. Are you?" Richard leaned his elbows on the table, giving Dylan all of his attention.

"We're very happy here, but Maggie's still busy learning all about being a witch and I'm planning on taking over kitchen duties when our chef leaves in a few months. He's been teaching me everything he knows so it will be a seamless transition."

"I see. That appears to be a good path. I hope you'll plan a trip back in time to visit with us. We'd love to have you."

"We've actually been talking about it. We'll have to coordinate our schedules with Edna, but we definitely want to." Maggie glanced at Dylan who nodded his agreement.

"Good. I look forward to it. Now, if you'll excuse me, I'm going to see if my wife is awake yet. We wish to explore Glendaloch. It will be a pleasure to do it as a law abiding man." He chuckled as he stood and left them to their breakfast.

"It's so wonderful getting to visit with everyone," Dylan said. He sipped his coffee and smiled.

"It is. I'm especially happy to see Jenna and Cormac," Maggie said.

"She's really bummed that she hasn't been able to get pregnant."

"Maybe that will change while they're here." Maggie shrugged and continued eating.

"Do you know something I don't?" Dylan raised an eyebrow in her direction.

Maggie rolled her eyes at his question.

"That's not an answer," he said.

"Well, it should be." She giggled as she poured more coffee

into his cup.

"Don't be keeping any witchy secrets from me. I am your husband after all."

"There's nothing to tell at the moment. I promise."

"But you will when there is?"

Maggie stood, walked behind Dylan's chair, and wrapped her arms around his shoulders, kissing his cheek. "Ye'll be the first to know, but I will tell ye I'm nae in the business of impregnating women."

Dylan laughed and pulled her around into his lap. "Have I told you how much I love you?"

"I believe ye've told me and shown me," Maggie managed before Dylan captured her mouth in a sweet, sensual kiss.

"Mmm… I could do this all day, but we've got company to take care of."

"Other than Richard, I haven't seen anyone up and about. It's just you and me baby."

"And we have things to do."

"Maggie, you're killing me. Come on." He stood, picking her up in the process.

She was just reconsidering, when the front door of the inn opened and the sounds of cheery voices came their way. "I guess ye'll have to put me down. It sounds like the breakfast crowd is coming."

Dylan nipped at her earlobe. "Later. You're mine," he whispered as he carefully put her down.

"Happily yers." She kissed him and then reluctantly stepped away to greet their guests.

"Good morning!" Cailin said as they hurried into the dining room.

"Good morning," Dylan answered. "Where are you all coming from?"

"We went for a walk," Ashley said. "I love Glendaloch. It's such a pretty little village." She shot Cailin a look and he deftly ignored it. She was trying to get him to agree to stay in Glendaloch. She'd feel a lot better about Emma's health if they were somewhere with modern medicine. He wasn't very keen on the idea. She was going to have to work on him, but if she had her way, they wouldn't be returning to Breaghacraig with the others.

"May I?" Maggie held out her arms to take Emma from Ashley.

"Of course." Ashley handed Emma to Maggie. "She looks a little warm. Do you think she has a fever?"

Maggie touched a hand to the baby's face. "No. She feels pretty cool to me."

"Ashley, Emma's fine. Don't worry so much." Jenna put a comforting hand on her friend's arm. "Besides, we're going to go see Dr. Ferguson later, remember."

Ashley smiled somewhat reluctantly at her friend. "What's for breakfast?" she asked. She really needed to get a grip. She knew she was over reacting to everything when it came to Emma, but she didn't know how to stop herself. The stress she'd been feeling over the last months was almost unbearable. The others all tried their best to put her fears at ease, but it wasn't working. She'd speak with Dr. Ferguson about it. He'd know what to do. Ashley took a seat at the table and Cailin put his hands on her shoulders. She knew she had to be stressing him out too, but he never lost patience with her, instead using reason to put her fears to rest.

MAGGIE AND DYLAN were both fascinated with Emma. She had a tight grip on Dylan's pinky finger and examined both their faces with an intent gaze.

"Isn't she beautiful?" Maggie asked.

"Very," Dylan answered. "Are you sure you don't want one?"

"Dylan. We've talked about this. Not yet."

"Okay. Okay. It's just that you look so natural holding her."

"Just because I know how to hold a baby and I'm loving every minute of it doesn't mean I'm ready to have a baby... yet."

Dylan dropped the subject. "I set up a buffet, so grab your dish and get something to eat."

Ashley, Cailin, Jenna and Cormac all headed to the food, just as Robert, Irene and the children came downstairs. "I thought I smelled something good," Robert said as he grabbed a dish. Irene gave each of the children one and took one for herself. They lined up between their parents who served each of them and then sent them to sit at the table.

"So what's everyone up to today?" Dylan asked as he poured coffee into Cailin's mug.

"We're going to have breakfast and then a visit with Dr. Ferguson," Cormac said.

"After that I think Edna said something about shopping," Ashley said.

Ewan entered the dining room alone. "Good morning."

"Where's Lena," Maggie asked.

"She's gone to breakfast with an old friend."

Dylan noted from Ewan's tone and demeanor that he wasn't terribly happy about it. "Is everything okay, Ewan."

Ewan harrumphed and got himself a plate.

The others all exchanged concerned glances.

"I can see yer troubled, brother," Robert said.

"Aye. I am." Ewan filled his plate and then returned to the table. "Lena has gone to breakfast with a man. She says he is an old friend, but I get the feeling there's more to it than that."

"Lena loves ye verra much, Ewan," Irene added. "She must have many old friends here. This is where she grew up."

"I ken it, but I saw the way this man looked at her."

"She did have a life before she me ye," Maggie said. "He's probably an old boyfriend."

Ewan practically dropped his fork on hearing this.

"Don't worry, Ewan. Don't ye have any old loves that Lena doesn't know about."

He thought about this for a moment. "Aye. I do. But I would never place myself in the position of dining alone with them."

"Did ye tell her how ye felt?"

"Nae. I didnae."

"So ye expect her to be able to read yer mind?"

"I see yer point, but she's gone now and I cannae tell her."

"She's just having breakfast, she's not planning to leave ye and move back to Glendaloch."

Ewan looked miserable and Dylan felt his pain. Maggie was right though. "She'll be back soon, man. Ye'll see. Everything will be fine."

Lena met Michael at Sarah's Bakery and Tea Shop just down the street from the inn.

"Lena, it's so good to see ye." Michael leaned in and kissed her cheek.

She felt a little awkward about the meeting. She could tell that Ewan was not at all happy about it, but she had promised to meet Michael and so here she was.

"Thank ye for being open to breakfast instead of lunch or dinner. I'm visiting with my husband and children and this works better for me."

"I'm happy to see ye, Lena." Michael was staring at her and it was making her quite uncomfortable.

"Michael, I'm sorry. I'm sorry that I walked away that day all those years ago and left ye without a word."

"Why did ye go, Lena?"

"Curiosity. Glendaloch is the perfect place to grow up, but I wanted more. I wanted to have an adventure and that's exactly what happened."

"Ye were my first love, Lena and as such, I've never forgotten ye."

Lena didn't know what to say. She'd already apologized, but somehow that simply wasn't enough.

"I waited and waited for ye to return, Lena and when ye didnae I got on with my life." He took her hand. "Yer even more beautiful, if that's possible."

Lena snatched her hand back. "Michael. I dinnae ken what it is ye wish to come from this meeting, but I'm a most happily married woman. What we had was a childhood romance."

"I apologize. I'm not doing a very good job of expressing myself. I wanted ye to know that I'm alright. I've married and I have a little girl. We recently moved back here to Glendaloch. Ye see, when ye left I was devastated, but if ye hadnae left I would never have found the courage to leave Glendaloch. I went off to school. I got my degree and I met my wife. While ye were my first love, she is my forever love. Much as I'm sure Ewan is yers."

Lena didn't know what to say. She had assumed his intentions were to win her back and she'd gotten it all terribly wrong.

"When I took yer hand, I was taking the hand of the girl I knew growing up. When I told ye were beautiful, I meant it. Ye are a beauty. But me heart is no longer yers. I wished to meet ye as a friend, Lena. Nothing more."

Lena breathed a sigh of relief. "Well, I'm sure I must seem quite the idjit."

"Not at all. I've never been verra good at expressing my thoughts in a way that makes sense. I thought I'd perhaps improved over the years, but I can see that I havenae."

"We'll leave it at that then. I'm starving. Can we order some breakfast please?"

"That's why we're here after all."

Lena rushed back to the inn. She had a wonderful breakfast with Michael and after their initial awkwardness it had gone very smoothly. They'd spent the majority of their time talking about their children and spouses. As it turned out, it had been very good to see him and she would count him a lifelong friend. They'd already decided that the next time she was back in town their families would get together for a visit.

Much to Lena's surprise, Ewan was waiting for her. He stood leaning against the front wall of the inn, looking as handsome as he always did. Her heart skipped a beat at the sight of him and she ran straight into his arms.

"Lena, are ye back so soon?" he asked.

"Ye can see that I am. Yes. I had a lovely breakfast with my good friend Michael, but I'm happy to be back here to spend the rest of my day and life with ye."

Ewan smiled that slow, sexy smile she loved, tipping her chin up with his finger to cover her lips with his in a long, slow kiss.

"You two love to kiss out in public, don't you," Dylan said as he opened the door. "Seriously, everyone in Glendaloch is going to have something to say about this."

Ewan didn't let go of Lena, chuckling softly in response to Dylan. "Come my love, if ye plan to spend the rest of yer life with me, we'd best begin."

CHAPTER 7

ANGELINA & RICHARD

"GOOD MORNING, MY love." Richard planted a loving kiss on Angelina's cheek.

She stretched and yawned, turning away. "Can I sleep a little longer, please."

Richard knew her well. She always attempted to squeeze a few more minutes of sleep in before rising. He chuckled softly. "Do you really wish to waste time sleeping when we could be out and about enjoying our visit to Glendaloch."

"You're really excited to be here, aren't you?"

"I am. I did spend some time here before I met you my love and I'd like to share it with you. I'd also like to take young Henry to see Dr. Ferguson while we're here."

"Oh, good idea. We should have him take a look at all of us."

"We can do that if you like, but you need to get up first."

"Alright, alright. I'm getting up. Henry's still sleeping. Such a good baby. He only woke up once last night."

"We are blessed." Richard cradled Angelina's face in his hands and took in her beauty. "I'll see to Henry. You take your time rising and then we'll go downstairs for something to eat."

Richard was a very hands-on father, as Angelina called it. He had never felt terribly close with his own, but Henry would have a father who showed him how much he was loved. No pressure would be placed on his son to be someone other than the man he was meant to be. He went to the cradle, peeking in to see Henry staring up at him. He had his mother's blue eyes, which pleased

Richard to no end. "Hello, my son."

Henry's face softened at the sound of Richard's voice. He smiled and Richard marveled at that small accomplishment. "He's smiling at me. I think he loves me."

"I think he does too. He has the best father in the whole wide world." Angelina was up and standing behind him now. Her long black hair cascaded in a waterfall of darkness around her lovely face. She placed her hands on Richard's waist and he moved slightly so she could peek around him to look adoringly on her son. "Do you think your mother would like to join us when we see Dr. Ferguson?"

"I'm sure she would. She's fascinated by everything she's seen so far. Undoubtedly she'd enjoy the opportunity to see a doctor's office."

"Dr. Ferguson will be happy to know he has so many more than willing patients who can't wait to see him," she said with a giggle.

Richard picked up Henry and handed him to Angelina for his feeding. "I'll go get mother." He slipped from the room and knocked on Lady Catherine's door. There was no answer, so he opened it to see that she was already up and gone. He headed back downstairs where he found her helping herself to breakfast. Ashley, Cailin, Jenna and Cormac were also seated and eating. "Good morning," he said.

"Good morning," Ashley said as she glanced up from her food giving him a warm smile. "How are you? Did you sleep well?"

"I'm fine, thank you and I did sleep very well. Angelina is feeding Henry and then she'll be down for her own breakfast." He noted that Emma was cradled in her father's arm, while he ate with the other. "Mother, we're going to stop in and see my friend Dr. Ferguson today. Would you like to join us?"

Lady Catherine placed her plate on the table next to Jenna. "I would. How do you know this Dr. Ferguson?"

Richard didn't wish to bring up a sore subject that might cause Ashley distress, but he hoped she'd be alright with what little he would say. "I stayed with him when I visited Glendaloch the last time." He made a quick check of Ashley's reaction, but she was busy eating and didn't seem at all phased by what he'd just said. She had forgiven him and was willing to put those days in the past.

"When ye go, Richard, can ye tell him that we all would like to come in to see him as well?" Cailin said, motioning to include his wife as well as Jenna and Cormac.

"I would be happy to," Richard replied. He made himself a plate of food from the buffet and sat next to his mother, who seemed to be enjoying Dylan's breakfast creation. "As soon as we've all eaten, we'll go," he said to Lady Catherine.

AFTER FEEDING HENRY and getting herself dressed, Angelina bundled him up snuggly for their journey to Dr. Ferguson's. "Come, my little man. Let's go get your father and grandmother."

She headed downstairs where she found everyone done with their breakfast. "Are you ready to go?" she asked Richard.

"We've just finished. Don't you want something to eat?" Richard seemed concerned.

"I'm not really that hungry. I'll just grab a scone and we can be on our way." She handed the baby to Lady Catherine who was holding out her arms and then headed to the buffet where she grabbed a napkin and a scone. "Mmmm… this is really good," she said after taking a bite. "Let's go. We'll see you all later."

She was dressed in a comfortable pair of jeans and a sweater, provided by Edna. Everyone was dressed in twenty first century garb, with the exception of Lady Catherine. She had no interest in trying on or wearing anything other than her own clothing. Richard got his mother's cloak and Angelina's jacket from the coat rack and helped them each into them. He then put on the black leather jacket Edna gave him. Angelina whistled her appreciation. When she'd met him in San Francisco, she'd loved the way he looked in a very similar jacket. "Sexy," she whispered into his ear as she planted a kiss on his cheek, causing Richard to pause in his progress towards the front door. His dark gaze sent chills of delight across her body. She couldn't wait to be alone with him later in the day.

The walk to Dr. Ferguson's office wasn't so very far. Glendaloch proper consisted of one main street, with most residents living above their own shops or a little further afield like Mrs. MacDougall. Richard had to laugh as he recognized himself in his mother's behavior.

"I want to remember every detail of this wonderful place." She examined everything from the storefront windows to the goods behind them. The cars fascinated her, much as they had Richard. "What are those called again, Angelina?"

"Those are cars, or automobiles, Catherine." Angelina and Lady Catherine had made fast friends when she'd arrived at his home and they spent much of their time together working on the vineyard that Angelina had decided to start. Richard had never considered doing any such thing. He'd always been happy to buy his wine while he was in London, but Angelina convinced him, and she was right, that if they made their own wine they would never have to drink spoiled wine again. Their vineyards were doing exceptionally well thanks to both of the women in his life. And they weren't they only thing thriving. Lady Catherine had a new purpose in life. He could see the glow in her face and hear it in her excited words when she spoke of what they'd accomplished. She was also being transformed into a woman of business. Angelina had taught her well and she could negotiate a tough price with the best of them.

"Richard, on the way back, let's stop in the bookstore we just passed."

"I think that would be a great place to explore, especially for you, Mother."

"I agree." Richard noted that she seemed tense. "Will this Dr.

Ferguson think it strange that I'm dressed this way?"

"Dr. Ferguson is aware of the bridge and the time travelers. He will not question it at all."

"Good." Her shoulders relaxed as did her gait.

Stopping in front of a building similar in construction to the inn, Richard opened the door for the women and followed them in. A wood paneled sitting room with a large red and blue oriental carpet on the floor was lined with empty wooden chairs. A clock atop the fireplace tick-tocked loudly in the silence.

"Dr. Ferguson?" Richard called into the room beyond them. "Dr. Ferguson?"

"Just a moment. I'll be right there." They could hear the clinking of glass in the background and before long, Dr. Ferguson emerged from the curtained doorway to greet them. "As I live and breathe. Is it really ye, Richard?" Not waiting for an answer, the man strode to Richard, throwing his arms around him in greeting.

"It is I," Richard responded, grinning like a fool.

"Good, because I don't make it a habit of hugging strangers here in my waiting room." He slapped Richard on the back before turning to Angelina and Lady Catherine who were smiling broadly at the scene. "And who have we here?"

"This is my wife, Angelina, and my son, Henry."

"I'm so pleased to make yer acquaintance and I'm pleased that our Richard has found love with such a beauty. And Henry. A classic name that suits him well." Dr. Ferguson turned to Lady Catherine with a look of appreciation. "And who is this lovely creature?"

"This is my mother, Lady Catherine."

She curtsied as if she were meeting the king and the good doctor was more than charmed. Richard exchanged a grin with his wife, noting that he wasn't the only one who noticed their instant connection.

"It's good to see you again, Dr. Ferguson," Richard said.

"Please call me Arthur, Richard. We're old friends, arenae we?"

"Yes. You're right. It's just been a long time since I've seen you.

You look good."

"I have to. Being the doctor here in Glendaloch, if I didn't always look the picture of health, my patients might get worried." He chuckled and turned to Catherine. "Please come sit." He took her hand and led her to one of the chairs. "These arenae verra comfortable, I know, but I wasnae prepared for company. My apartments are upstairs over my office and I'm afraid I'm not the tidiest man. Richard can attest to that."

"I don't recall. I was only ever happy to have a friend here in this time."

"Yer a good man, Richard and ye were a good guest."

"Thank you for believing in me. It means more than you can know."

"So yer a father and husband now. Good for ye."

"Arthur, can I impose upon you to have a look at my son? He's been healthy so far, but I know in this time your medicine is far ahead of that which we live with in my time."

"I'd be happy to. I'll do a general exam on all of ye, if ye don't mind."

"Thank you, Dr. Ferguson," Angelina said.

Lady Catherine was mesmerized, it seemed, by the good doctor. She hadn't so much as looked at another man since his father had passed all those years ago. "Yes. Thank you," she managed to mutter.

CHAPTER 8

"THE FOUR MUSKETEERS," Jenna laughed as she, Ashley and their husbands headed down the street arm in arm. Emma was in a pouch, snuggled up to Cailin's chest. Edna had surprised them with it after their arrival and Ashley was so happy she had. Cailin loved it. He could have both hands free and yet still enjoy his baby cuddled close.

"I realize we can't bring this back with us, but mayhap we could make something similar?" Cailin glanced down at Ashley and she smiled sweetly back at him.

"Of course we can. Give me some fabric and a needle and thread and I can make something that will work just as well." Her mood was much lighter this morning. Her apprehension about Emma having a fever had waned when everyone had reassured her that she was just fine and now she was heading off to see Dr. Ferguson who would surely agree with her that it was better to raise Emma in the twenty-first century. As much as she loved Breaghacraig and all its residents, she couldn't risk losing her baby to some childhood illness that was no longer in existence in this time.

As they approached Dr. Ferguson's office, they noticed Richard, Angelina and Lady Catherine exiting with Henry.

"Good morning, again." Richard smiled warmly at them. "Dr. Ferguson is expecting your visit."

"How'd everything go?" Jenna asked.

"Fine. We're all in the best of health, including little Henry."

"Don't you worry about him getting sick back at home?" Ashley directed her question to Angelina. She assumed she must be feeling the same level of anxiety that she was.

"No. Not really. Henry's been surprisingly healthy so far. Besides, I'd be willing to bet that if we needed to, Edna would help us get back here to see Dr. Ferguson, so I'm not worried at all."

Ashley didn't respond. She wished she could let this go. It would make things so much easier for her and for Cailin. She didn't want to force him to stay in Glendaloch. She only hoped Dr. Ferguson would be her ally in this.

"We'll see you later then. Edna has some shopping planned for all of us this afternoon."

They waved goodbye and entered Dr. Ferguson's office door. He was standing there waiting for them.

"Hello, all." Dr. Ferguson greeted them with a warm smile. "Welcome, welcome."

"Hi Dr. Ferguson. Thanks so much for making time for us while we're here."

"It's my pleasure. I just did the exact same thing for Richard and his family. Shall we take a look at the baby first?"

"Please," Ashley rushed to his side and he escorted her to the exam room followed closely by Cailin.

"So, do ye have anything in particular that yer concerned about?"

Cailin glanced at Ashley and nodded for her to take the lead. "Well, pretty much everything. I'm worried that living in the sixteenth century isn't going to be a good thing. I think we should move back here where Emma will have access to a doctor and modern medicine."

Dr. Ferguson took Emma from Cailin and laid her down on the exam table. "She looks the picture of health." He picked her up and placed her on the baby scale. "She falls right where we would expect her to be. Sixteen pounds and her height looks to be about twenty-six inches. Perfect." He looked in her eyes, her ears, and her mouth. Everything looks good as far as I can see."

Ashley was relieved. "But you think we should move back

here, don't you?"

"Nay. There's no need. I'm sure Edna would whisk ye back to see me if there were any emergencies. Yer fine to stay where ye are. Now, let me have a look at ye."

Dr. Ferguson, took his time examining both Ashley and Cailin and asking them lots of questions. When he was finished, he turned to Ashley. "My dear, I know ye have some anxiety about all of this, but ye need to relax and stop worrying about every little thing. New parents are prone to over worrying and, my dear, ye have tipped that scale. I'd like ye to take some time for yerself. Every day. Go for a walk, get outside. Let someone else take care of Emma for a little while. Yer big, strong husband here would be happy to help ye, I'm sure."

"I would, Dr. Ferguson, if she'd let me."

"Ashley, 'tis for yer own good and the bairn's."

"I know it is, Dr. Ferguson. I just have this terrible feeling that something bad is going to happen and I can't get it out of my head."

"Cailin, yer going to have to insist on her getting some relaxation."

"I will, sir. Thank ye."

"Alright, let me see Jenna and Cormac then." He guided them out the door of the exam room. "I've been invited to Christmas Eve dinner, so I'll see ye both there."

"I HAVEN'T BEEN able to get pregnant," Jenna blurted out as soon as Dr. Ferguson asked her how she was feeling.

"I see."

"We've been trying for months and nothing. I think there must be something wrong with me."

"Of course there's always the possibility that there is some reason that ye cannae get pregnant, but I'd say that ye need to take yer time and see what happens. Yer both healthy adults. I'll need to examine ye both but without doing more elaborate testing, which cannae be done here in my office, there's no way I can be sure why yer having this problem. What I can tell ye is that yer nae the first young couple I've seen who are concerned about not conceiving. In many cases, it just takes more time than ye've given it. My suggestion would be to stop worrying about it and simply enjoy being a couple who love each other. The baby will come soon enough, ye'll see."

"Thank ye, sir." Cormac placed an arm around his wife. "Tis what I've been telling ye all along, love."

"I know. I only want to have what everyone else has. I know you want it too and it's been breaking my heart that I can't give it to you."

"'Tis nae yer fault. I love ye, Jenna - with or without a bairn."

"Love is a wonderful thing, isnae it? I have a sneaking suspicion that the next time we meet, ye'll have yer wish. If not, come back here next year and we'll arrange those tests I mentioned." He patted Cormac on the back. "Now. Let's get those exams out of the way, shall we?"

"Do you feel better about things?" Ashley asked as they waved goodbye to the good doctor.

"Surprisingly I do. He put me at ease and I'm not going to worry about the future. I'm going to focus on living each day as it comes and loving my husband as much as I can, because without him I'd be lost."

"I know what you mean. I've got to seriously get a grip on being the over protective mother. I'll be happy to remind you to live in the moment, if you'll remind me not to be so obsessive about Emma's health."

"Agreed. I'm happy we have each other." The two women locked arms and walked ahead of their husbands and Emma. The men were having an animated conversation about whether or not Cailin's

Glendaloch was better than Cormac's San Francisco.

Jenna and Ashley couldn't help but giggle at what they were overhearing.

"Cailin, I tell ye, San Francisco is a much more wondrous place. Glendaloch has only the one bridge, but San Francisco has two and they're much bigger. And Glendaloch has only the one street. San Francisco is vast. There are cars, buses and trains. There are many, many more people, everywhere ye go."

"I like Glendaloch. 'Tis better," Cailin protested.

"Ye wouldnae ken better if it bit ye in the arse," Cormac teased.

The men had picked up some of their wives favorite sayings and liked to use them whenever there was an opportunity.

"Brother, I'd nae be so quick to choose a battle of wits. Ye ken I'd win." Ashley could tell Cailin was controlling his temper.

"If ye had any wits I might be worried," Cormac responded.

"Stop it, you two." Jenna turned back to reprimand them. "Does the sibling rivalry ever stop?"

"'Tis all in good fun. We've been at each other since we were wee ones and we still love each other." Cormac threw an arm over Cailin's shoulder, kissing his brother's cheek.

"'Tis yer good luck that I've Emma in me arms or I'd…"

"Or ye'd what? Kiss me back?" Cormac chuckled. "Or maybe kiss me arse?"

Ashley rolled her eyes. She knew this kind of teasing could go on for hours. Cormac was an expert at getting under Cailin's skin, but he was right about the fact that they loved each other and she loved that about them. Cailin was the serious older brother and Cormac was the light-hearted younger brother. No matter the circumstance, they always were there to support each other. Even better than that was the fact that her best friend, Jenna, was now her sister-in-law. Cormac was as perfect for her as Cailin was for Ashley.

CORMAC WISHED TO hold wee Emma more than anything, but he feared it would only cause Jenna to gaze on him with those sad eyes she showed him whenever he played with his nieces and nephews. He loved them all so very much and he was sure it must be obvious to his wife that it was the one thing missing in what he felt was an already perfect life. Yes, of course, he wanted a bairn of his own. He hoped that their visit to Dr. Ferguson had put her mind at ease and that she would stop being obsessed by their inability to have a baby. Cormac was sure it would happen in due time, but until then he would keep his longing for a son or daughter to himself, not wishing to cause Jenna more grief. Truth be told, his beautiful wife was all he really needed, and come what may, bairn or no bairn he was a very happy man.

CHAPTER 9

EDNA SLEPT BETTER last night than she had in years. Something about having all of her time traveling family here at the inn put her mind to rest. She'd never admit to anyone, including Angus, how much she worried about these people she'd come to know and love so much. Yes, she'd sleep well while they were at The Thistle & Hive.

She rose from bed and headed straight for the dining room where Dylan had laid out a sumptuous breakfast for their guests. Having Dylan and Maggie living here at the inn had given her some breathing room. She no longer had to do it all. Not in the witchcraft department and not in the running of the inn. Angus had always done his best to help her, but there were some things he just wasn't good with. He was not a witch, so he couldn't help her with the bridge. He did help with the inn, although one look at him sometimes scared the guests away before they even registered. They had no idea he was actually a teddy bear in disguise.

She smiled, thinking of her handsome Highlander. Angus loved her and her quirkiness, showing her every day why she was the luckiest woman on earth.

"Edna, I've put together a plate of all yer favorites," Angus said, patting the seat next to him. "Come sit down."

"Thank ye, my love." Edna kissed his cheek as she took her seat. "What have ye planned for the day?"

"Breakfast." Angus continued eating. "Dylan is a fine chef. He'll be a good replacement for John."

"Do ye think ye should perhaps show the lads around while I

take the lasses shopping?" Occasionally Edna had to push Angus to be more social.

"If they wish. They havenae asked me."

"Ye cannae wait for them to ask, ye big fool."

Angus eyed her with feigned hurt. "How can ye call me a big fool? Am I nae the man ye love?" He pouted and Edna couldn't help but laugh.

"Aye. Ye are the one and only man I love and have ever loved. I ken ye'd like to sit here and read or spar with yer hay bale warrior out back, but our guests are only here for a few days. They're not staying like ye did, so it would be nice if ye could show them around."

"As ye wish, my love. I've nae seen ye so excited and ye slept well last night, didnae ye."

"I did, Angus. I feel relieved to have them here with me. It's hard to explain, but knowing where they are and that they arenae in any danger means the world to me. 'Tis like they're all my children."

"I ken yer meaning and I'm happy that even if 'tis only for a short while, yer mind can rest easy." His large hand rubbed her back. Warmth, comfort, and love were all transmitted in that small gesture. Edna smiled as she relaxed even more and took the first bite of her meal.

Angus would never tell Edna this, but he worried about her just about as much as she worried about their guests, if not more. He wanted her to be this happy and relaxed all the time. He hoped to convince her to take a much needed vacation after the holidays, perhaps to Spain or Italy. It would take some work, but now that Maggie and Dylan were with them, he hoped she could relinquish her duties for a week or two.

He finished his breakfast and watched as Edna daintily picked up a piece of toast and took a bite. His fingers were drawn to the blue streak in her hair, which had fallen into her face. He gently tucked it behind her ear, brushing her cheek with his knuckles as he did so. Edna rewarded him with a loving smile, which lit the emerald green eyes he cherished.

"It appears it may snow later today," Edna said. "I'm going to take the lasses shopping for Christmas gifts. Maybe ye should do the same with the gents. We can meet for lunch at the pub."

"Who will watch the wee ones?"

"Teddy can watch them."

"Teddy? Do ye believe 'tis a good idea?"

"Aye. He'll be fine. I ken they are a handful, but Teddy can handle it. They'll be here at the inn. If he needs our help, he can call us on the cell phone. We're only moments away."

"I'd like to see ye convince young Ashley of that."

"She's a new mother and, yes, she's a bit overprotective, but this will be a good time for her to place some trust in others." Edna put down her fork and faced Angus. "They're off to see Dr. Ferguson ye ken. I'm hoping he'll put her mind at ease about Emma's health. I'd like to find a way to help with that when she returns to Breaghacraig."

"I'm sure ye'll think of something," Angus winked. His belief in Edna and her ability to make any situation right was evident. Occasionally the way she reached her goal was a little worrisome, but things always ended up exactly where she wanted them to be.

"Alright then. I'll take the men shopping as ye wish, but if they're anything like me, they'll nae be verra excited about it."

Edna's joy at his pronouncement seemed to light up her face, which made Angus feel quite good about his decision. He'd do anything for Edna, even go shopping.

EDNA WAS JUST finishing up her breakfast when the door opened and Richard, Angelina, Lady Catherine and Henry returned.

"Good morning," Edna said. "Have ye eaten?"

"Aye. We ate before we went out."

"How was yer visit with the doctor?"

"'Twas good. Everyone is healthy and we've nothing to worry over."

"Once everyone is back, we'll go do some Christmas shopping. How does that sound?"

"Like music to my ears," Angelina said. "I'm going up to the room for a minute. Henry needs to be fed."

"I'll join you, love." Richard followed Angelina upstairs, leaving Lady Catherine behind.

"Catherine, come sit with me." Edna motioned to the chair next to her. "Angus is getting ready for our outing and I've some time to sit and relax. How are ye enjoying yer stay?"

"Edna, I cannot thank you enough for welcoming us into your home. It's an adventure I wouldn't miss."

"How was yer visit with Dr. Ferguson?" Edna watched closely as Catherine's face lit up at the mention of his name.

"Very nice. He is a good man, and a handsome one at that." Catherine's face turned two or three shades of pink with that pronouncement. "I'm thankful that he befriended Richard. I'm also aware that you had a lot to do with helping him realize the man he was truly meant to be."

"I cannae help meself, Catherine. I'm a meddler at heart and Richard seemed as though he needed an opportunity to be redeemed. I sent him off on a journey of discovery, but he did all the hard work. I'm so happy for all of ye." Edna sipped her tea and then grabbed another cup, which she filled for Catherine. "Now tell me all about Dr. Ferguson."

"It's been quite some time since my husband died and I've not been at all interested in finding a new man to fill his shoes. He was a difficult man and I didn't wish to put myself in the position of dealing with that ever again. Dr. Ferguson is a kind and gentle man. Nothing at all like Richard's father. If there were someone like him in my time, I'd be happy to be a married lady again."

Meddlesome Edna was itching to do some matchmaking, but even she was unsure how she could make this work out. "One never knows, Catherine, the right man will find his way to ye."

"Do you see it, Edna. Richard told me that you have the sight."

"I don't see it as much as know it." How could she explain to Catherine that she would most likely be meddling in her life in the near future? "'Tis too difficult to explain, but in yer case I cannae see the future." *But I can help mold the future.*

Lady Catherine appeared disappointed. "I don't know why I'm so interested in finding love after all this time, but perhaps it's best to leave things as they are. I have a good life with Richard and Angelina. My grandson Henry is the love of my life now."

"Ye have another son, don't ye?" Edna asked.

"Yes. Edward. He's Richard's younger brother." Catherine responded.

"Is he married?"

"No. He hasn't fallen in love yet."

"So, ye dinnae believe in marrying for lands and title then."

"No. Not at all. I wish I had married for love, but then I wouldn't have Richard and Edward, would I?"

"Life can be a puzzle, Catherine. Don't give up on love. It may find ye yet."

EDNA AND ANGUS stood surrounded by their guests as they got ready to go out. Ashley appeared quite anxious about leaving Emma with Teddy. Cailin practically had to pry the babe out of her arms.

"Don't worry, Ashley. We're not going far. We are in Glendaloch after all. How far can we go?" Edna chuckled at this. "Teddy can manage the children just fine. He'll call me if there's any problem and we can be back here in minutes."

"But Angelina is taking little Henry," she protested.

"Only because he needs to be fed more frequently. If I could, I'd be happy to leave him with Teddy." Edna nodded her thanks to Angelina for helping.

Ashley glanced Teddy's way and he gave her what amounted to a very shy smile. Edna could see Ashley gathering her courage. "Alright. Teddy I know you'll take good care of Emma. Everything you need is right here in this bag." She hurriedly handed the baby to him and turned away.

Edna could see that she was trying really hard to be brave and that they needed to depart as quickly as possible before Ashley changed her mind. "Shall we?" she said as she motioned to the door.

Cailin tucked Ashley into his side. "Come, love. 'Twill be good to get away. Remember what Dr. Ferguson told ye."

Ashley didn't answer and Cailin led her through the door and onto the sidewalk.

"Ladies, ye'll be coming with me and lads, ye'll go with Angus. This way ye can purchase gifts for each other without the other knowing what yer getting for them." She turned and headed down the street, indicating with a nod of her head that Angus should go the other way. As she walked, she could hear Angus hemming and hawing over what he was telling the men.

"Come on, lads. I dinnae ken how ye feel about this, but the Mrs. has spoken. She wants us to shop and shopping is what we'll do."

CHAPTER 10

TEDDY & THE CHILDREN

TEDDY SAT IN his usual corner at The Thistle & Hive Inn, keeping an eye on the children - all seven of them, including baby Emma who lay on the floor in the midst of her cousins and Chester. He was babysitting unbeknownst to the children. Wee Robert thought himself big enough to be in charge and so his elders humored him by letting him think he was the one protecting the children. Their parents were all out doing some last minute Christmas shopping for them and in order to keep their gifts a surprise, wanted to go on their own. Edna assured everyone that Teddy would keep an eagle eye on them and so they had nothing to worry about, but Teddy found himself getting sleepy. He'd been seated in the same spot for hours and the warmth from the fireplace was affecting his ability to stay awake. He'd nodded off and jerked awake more times than he could count. He couldn't fight it another minute and closing his eyes, drifted off.

WEE ROBERT HAD been watching Teddy out of the corner of his eye. Although his parents had left him in charge, he knew that it was really Teddy who was supposed to be in charge of them and he wasn't very happy about it. He was just waiting for his chance and as luck would have it, he noticed Teddy was nodding off and decided at that very moment it would be a good idea for the children to go out for a walk to the stables.

"Ma, wouldnae like it, Robbie. We're to stay here until she returns." Fiona wrung her hands and looked at her brother with large, worried eyes.

"Da would expect me to see that me new horse was being cared for. We should all get our cloaks and walk to the stable. I ken the way, so there's nae need to worry, Fiona." Robert had given his son his very own pony a few weeks back and he had impressed upon him the importance of being responsible for his pony's well-being. Wee Robert wanted more than anything to show his Da that he had listened to him and if that meant taking his siblings for a walk to the stables to see that Tonn had been fed and watered, then that was what he was going to do.

"But 'tis cold outside, Robbie. What about baby Emma?" Fiona glanced the baby's way. Wee Robert could see she was still not convinced.

"We'll wrap her up in her blankets and I'll carry her. She'll be fine. Dinnae ye wish to see the horses? We can bring them carrots and apples from the kitchen." Robert waited for his sister's answer. He knew that if she didn't agree to go with him, that none of them would be going anywhere."

Fiona glanced across the room at Teddy. "Shoulnae we tell Teddy we're going?"

"Nae. He's so verra tired. He needs his rest." He was sure Teddy wouldn't allow them to go anywhere and he had decided that he must see Tonn.

"Can we take Chester with us then?" Fiona placed her wee hand on Chester's back and he turned to face her, planting a huge lick on her face. Fiona giggled and scrunching her face, backed away.

"Aye. Chester can come with us."

"Alright."

"We must be verra quiet though. We dinnae wish to awaken Teddy." Wee Robert held a finger to his lips as he gathered the other children together. Rowan and Ranald were always ready for an adventure, so it was all he could do to keep them from shrieking with joy and running out the door.

He carefully wrapped baby Emma in the blankets she was laying on and after they all had their cloaks secured, he picked her up and led the way through the doors to the kitchen. The staff at the inn were all at home with their own families, so no one was about. They took a basket from the counter and filled it with carrots and apples.

"Fiona, ye carry it, I've got Emma." Robert headed for the back door and the other children fell in line behind him. Fiona grabbed the basket and took up the rear. They quietly let themselves out and just as quietly closed the door behind them. "This way." Wee Robert led the way through the garden and down a pathway that went behind the buildings on the main street. They hadn't gone very far when they came across a red wagon. Robert placed Emma in the wagon, making sure she was safe. "Isobel, ye get in there with Emma. Yer too little to walk all the way." He helped her in and got her situated so that Emma's head was resting in her lap. He readjusted the blankets and then he grasped the handle of the wagon and pulled it behind himself as they trekked toward Mrs. MacDougall's stable.

It was only mid-day, but the sun was nowhere in sight. The sky was completely white with the promise of snow, which had Wee Robert walking a bit faster to get to the stables before it began. They were only about halfway there when the first flakes landed on them, at first softly, but soon the flakes became bigger and the snow fell faster.

"Robbie, we should go back," Fiona's tiny voice spoke from behind him.

"We're almost there, Fiona. Dinnae fash." He plodded along with purpose. He would see that they all arrived at the stable. It was only a short distance now. They had left the buildings of Glendaloch behind and they were now trudging along a path that was quickly being hidden by snow. He could barely see in front of his face, but he was sure they were headed in the right direction.

TEDDY AWOKE WITH a start. The room was silent and when he opened his eyes he had a moment of panic when he realized the children were gone. *They must be in their rooms.* He relaxed. He'd head up the stairs to check on them. Panic soon returned when he realized they weren't there. Edna would be very angry with him. He'd been given the responsibility of babysitting the children while their parents were out and he'd failed miserably. He ran back downstairs and into the kitchen. No one was about. Where could they be? Taking a deep breath and trying his best to calm his frazzled nerves, Teddy took a moment to think. If they were not inside then obviously they had gone out, but where. A quick glance out the window and his stomach dropped. There was a full scale blizzard taking place outside. He had to find them as soon as possible and hopefully before anyone was aware they were missing.

He grabbed his coat, a hat, put his boots on, and flew out the backdoor. He headed off through the garden and out the back gate. Left or right, which way should he turn. His eyes scanned both pathways. Fear gripped him as he thought he might not find them in time to save them from freezing to death. A small glimpse of orange was visible partially buried in the snow off to his left. Teddy hurried to the spot and bending to pick it up, he saw it was a carrot. Where were they going with a carrot? At least now he knew which direction they'd headed off in. Unfortunately, the snow, which was falling faster and faster had covered any tracks they may have left. Putting two and two together, Teddy surmised that they must be headed to Mrs. MacDougall's stables, possibly to feed the horses. He set off in that direction hoping the children made it before the snow became so thick that they lost their way. Blinded by the snow blowing in his face, Teddy ducked his head and pulled his jacket closer to stay warm. The wind was howling now in great gusts. He had to find them and get them back to the inn before any harm befell them and before their parents knew they were missing.

"How much farther do we have to go, Robbie?" Fiona's teeth chattered as she spoke.

"We're almost there." Wee Robert hoped he sounded convincing, because he wasn't so sure they were even headed in the right direction now. He had created a small tent over the top of baby Emma with an extra plaid he'd grabbed on the way out the inn door. Good thing he had, because otherwise she'd be covered in snow by now.

"Ye dinnae even know where we're going," Ranald shouted. "I'm going back to the inn." He turned and began stomping away.

"Ranald, wait. Ye'll get lost." Wee Robert was in charge. He was the oldest. The others *had* to listen to him. The others all stopped and watched as Ranald left.

"I'm going with him," Rowan said. "Ranald wait for me." He ran to catch up with his brother.

"Robbie, I'm cold. Can we go back too?" Fiona asked.

"We're almost there. It will take too long to walk back." He continued walking and pulling the wagon.

"But what of our cousins?" Fiona hesitated where she stood.

"I cannae stop them if they wish to go back, but we must hurry. Baby Emma must be getting cold." He hurried onward and his brother and sisters followed quietly behind. He gazed up to the heavens and said a silent prayer that they arrive at the stables safely, but he was beginning to have his doubts. They continued trudging through the snow, which was piling higher and higher by the minute. He checked back to see that everyone was still following along behind him and was relieved to see that other than the twins, his brother and sisters were still with him.

Rounding the next bend, his prayers were answered. The stable was right in front of them, decorated with lights and a large wreath over the doors. The snow had slowed them down and made their journey much longer than it should have. The weight of responsibility lifted slightly from his shoulders as they reached the closed stable doors. "Fiona, help me get these doors open." He lifted the cross bar that kept the doors secure and then as Fiona kicked at the pile of snow impeding their progress, Wee Robert pulled with all his might and finally the doors opened. He rushed everyone inside and was greeted by light and warmth.

"Who's there?" came a female voice from the rear of the stable. She spoke with the same accent as his Aunt Ashley and Aunt Jenna.

"'Tis I, Wee Robert and me brother and sisters. Oh, and me cousin baby Emma." He strained his eyes to see who it might be who was speaking to him, but there was no one there and they said nothing in response. "Fiona, we must close the doors."

They grasped the handles and shut the doors as best they could, then they headed towards the rear of the stable where Tonn's head peeked over the stable door. "Tonn, there ye be." Robbie went to his pony and blew gently into his nostrils. Tonn nickered to him and he reached into the basket of goodies and brought out a carrot, which he held out to his friend. Tonn happily gobbled it up, chewing quickly and making an orange foamy mess all around his mouth. The children all giggled at this.

Fiona looked under the blanket covering Emma, who had slept quite soundly while they walked. She now opened her eyes and taking one look at Fiona, began to cry loudly.

"Bring the little one here," came the voice from a stall further down the stable aisle way.

"Where are ye? Who are ye?" Wee Robert was frightened, but he didnae wish his siblings to see him that way, so he stood tall and began walking towards the voice.

CHAPTER 11

TEDDY WAS BEGINNING to lose hope that he'd locate the children. After finding the carrot, he'd seen nothing to indicate that they were heading along the path to the stables, but his intuition told him to keep going. The wind was blowing right in his face, causing him to look down and to the side to avoid the stinging snow. He carefully continued on his way using only the knowledge he'd garnered from years of living in Glendaloch. He'd walked this path many times and though he wasn't looking where he was going, he somehow knew the way. The tree stump he ran into, however, was not one he remembered ever seeing and much to his surprise, it spoke to him.

"Ow! Watch where yer going." The voice of a young boy yelled.

Teddy stopped and was shocked to see one of the twins. Gazing up he saw the other twin not far behind. "Where have ye been? I've been searching fer ye. Where are the others?" Teddy felt an odd combination of relief and panic on realizing that there were only two children in front of him.

"They went to see the horses. Ranald and I got tired of walking, so we turned around. I don't think they'll ever get there."

So the one he'd tripped over was Rowan. He'd had a devil of a time keeping them straight in his head. "Well, I'm sorry to tell ye this, Rowan, but we're heading back the way ye just came. Ye ken we must find them. We dinnae wish any harm to come their way." Teddy was surely using his daily allotment of words. He hardly ever had anything to say and he liked it that way. "Come along then."

"I'm so verra tired, Teddy. Do we have to go with ye?"

"Aye, ye do."

"Can ye carry us?" Two sets of pleading eyes gazed up at him. How could he refuse them?

Teddy reached his arms down and scooped up the two heavy bundles before continuing his walk. There was no way to avoid the snow hitting him in the face now. He'd best just get on with it, what good would it do him to complain? The only reason he found himself in this predicament was because he'd literally fallen asleep on the job. Edna would be very angry with him and he could only imagine how their parents would react.

"We're almost there, boys." Teddy wasn't sure if he was reassuring the twins or himself. Perhaps both. He could see the lights of Mrs. MacDougall's stables dimly shining through the falling snow. He picked up his pace and upon finally reaching the stable doors, he put the twins down and carefully opened them.

Teddy wasn't surprised to find the stable well-lit and warm. Mrs. MacDougall saw to it that every horse in her stable was well cared for and during the winter months that meant heating the space they called home. He was, however, surprised to see a woman he didn't recognize holding baby Emma and cooing softly to her.

"Teddy!" Fiona shouted, running to him. "Ye found us."

"Aye." He counted the children to make sure they were all present and accounted for. "Ye gave me quite a fright."

"We're sorry. Robbie wanted to come see his pony."

Wee Robert glanced sheepishly up at Teddy, not saying a word.

"And who is this?" Teddy motioned to the woman. Her head was covered with a hood, which cloaked her face in darkness. He couldn't see enough of her to decide if he knew her.

"My name's Marissa." She threw the hood back from her head, revealing bespectacled eyes of the brightest blue and a pert little turned up nose, all encased in a lovely heart shaped face, surrounded by platinum blonde hair, which was streaked much like Edna's only in pink. Her accent was distinctly American.

Teddy was immediately taken with her. In his eyes she was the most beautiful of women. He stammered and stuttered as he tried to speak, eventually managing, "I'm Teddy."

"You're the babysitter." She stated matter-of-factly.

"Aye. Not a verra good one, I'm afraid."

"These little rascals told me all about their adventure and for what it's worth, I don't see how anyone could blame you. They were pretty stealthy from what I understand. I'm just happy they made it to the stable before this little one turned into a popsicle." Marissa gazed down at Emma who beamed a smile that was filled with joy as she reached up a hand and grasped onto Marissa's hair.

Teddy moved closer under the pretense of seeing Emma. He stood as near to Marissa as he dared, wishing he was the one wrapping his hand in her hair. She smelled lovely too. An aroma of citrus and roses gently wafted through the air around her.

"These two must be Rowan and Ranald. I'm happy to see you didn't get lost on your way back to the inn."

"We werenae lost," Rowan stated. "Teddy made us come with him."

"Well, I'd say it was a good thing. Otherwise how would I have gotten to meet you?"

The twins softened, obviously as enchanted with Marissa as Teddy was. They too approached and stood as near as they could possibly get without dislodging Emma in the process.

"Shall we all sit down? I believe it will be a while before it's safe for you all to head back to the inn." Marissa carefully walked to the bales of straw neatly stacked against the back wall and sat on one at the bottom. The children followed suit, as did Teddy.

A door off to the side of the feed room opened revealing a startled Mrs. MacDougall. "What have we here?" she asked, smiling warmly at the children.

"We came to visit my Tonn," Wee Robert answered.

"Did ye now? 'Tis not the best day to be wandering about." She directed the last part of her comment to Teddy.

"'Tis a long story, Mrs. MacDougall," Teddy was embarrassed

once again at his failure.

"I know Teddy, and I've met Wee Robbie. I assume the rest of the children are visiting the inn, but I haven't had the pleasure of meeting this young lady." Mrs. MacDougall directed her attention to Marissa.

"I'm Marissa Merrivale." Marissa extended her free hand towards Mrs. MacDougall.

"Are ye visiting the inn as well?"

"Oh, no. I'm here in Scotland doing research for a book I'm writing. My rental car broke down and I was caught in the snow-storm. I was getting cold and tired and I needed shelter. I knocked on your door, but there wasn't any answer. I hope you don't mind that I let myself into the stable."

"Of course not. What kind of woman would I be to let ye freeze out there in this weather. Yer more than welcome to the warmth of the stable and the company ye seem to have found. I must have been upstairs. My hearing's not what it used to be. I'm sure that's why I missed yer knock." Mrs. MacDougall walked towards a large double door closet. "Teddy, would ye mind helping me?"

Teddy nodded and followed after her.

"I've got a table and some chairs here. I keep them for those rare occasions when someone wants to use my stable for a party. Here, Teddy, open this table up while I get out some chairs."

Teddy rolled the round table to a clear spot in the aisle way and unfolded the legs to set it upright. He then went back to retrieve the folding chairs Mrs. MacDougall was stacking along the wall.

"Teddy, ye get that all set up and I'll be right back." She was out the door in a flash. Teddy did as he was told and with the help of the children got all the chairs set up around the table.

A short while later, Mrs. MacDougall returned with a picnic basket and a large thermos. She handed Teddy a Christmas table cloth, which he put on the table. Next she placed dishes and cups out. Then came the treats. There were cookies in the shapes of rein-deer, Christmas trees, ornaments and wreaths all decorated with red and green frosting. Bowls of homemade candy came next, along with colorful candy canes. The children held back, but their eyes were wide with wonder at the sight of everything set out for them.

"Everyone sit." Mrs. MacDougall poured hot chocolate into their cups and then sat herself down next to Marissa. "May I?" she asked, nodding her head towards Emma.

"Of course." Marissa handed the baby over to her and then dug into the cookies, like a woman who hadn't eaten is a long while.

"Yer quite hungry, arenae ye?" Teddy asked. He found everything about her fascinating, including her appetite.

"I haven't eaten since yesterday."

Teddy exchanged a look with Mrs. MacDougall.

"My gosh, I'm being rude. I should probably slow down." She sat back in her chair and took a sip of the hot chocolate. "Mmmm…"

Teddy couldn't seem to take his eyes off of her. Mrs. MacDougall elbowed him in the side and aimed a sly wink his way. That was all it took for Teddy to avert his eyes and search the stable for something to take him away from her scrutiny. The horses would do. He rose and went down the aisle, stroking their velvety noses and ruffling their forelocks. He was embarrassed by his behavior. Granted he almost never met anyone who didn't live in Glendaloch and his experience with the opposite sex was very limited. Most of the lasses he knew treated him like their odd brother. He continued standing with his back to the group while he attempted to relax and get his emotions under control.

"Is EVERYTHING OKAY," Marissa asked. She could tell by his posture that he was attempting to hide from them.

Teddy stayed where he was, head tucked low. "Aye. Fine."

"Okay. I hope I didn't scare you away with the way I was eating. I mean, I know it was a bit over the top, but I was very hungry."

She was feeling embarrassed. She liked Teddy from the moment she first saw him and she was afraid that being herself in front of him would work like insect repellant on a mosquito. If it did, what could she do? She had long ago decided against pretense and instead had come to embrace her quirky side even though it did little to attract the opposite sex.

"I ken ye were. I just wished to see the horses, so I can reassure their owners that they are faring well." He slowly turned back towards them and gave himself a little shake before raising his head and attempting something that appeared to be a smile.

Marissa had all she could do to restrain the giggle that was bubbling in her throat. She glanced at Mrs. MacDougall who had obviously failed in that endeavor and who was now covering it up with a coughing fit into her napkin.

The children were happily eating their cookies and sipping their hot chocolate, unaware of the awkwardness that had suddenly descended on the adults.

"Where are ye from, Marissa?" Mrs. MacDougall lowered her napkin and smiled warmly at her.

"I'm from Boston." Marissa answered and then thinking perhaps she wouldn't know where Boston was added, "Massachusetts."

"Really? I have cousins who live there."

"I probably don't know them."

"I wouldn't imagine ye would. 'Tis a large city. Knowing everyone who resides there would take quite a bit of work on yer part." Mrs. MacDougall chuckled and put her napkin back in her lap.

That was quite a dumb thing to say. Of course this kind woman wouldn't think she knew her cousins. Marissa had always been a bit socially awkward, but she'd been working hard to be better in social situations. She obviously still had some work to do. "What part of the city do they live in?"

"Actually they live just outside of the city itself in a place called Somerville. Ye must be familiar with it."

"I am. I actually grew up there." She was about to continue, but

Teddy was back and had quietly taken his seat. There was something about him that Marissa found attractive. He definitely wouldn't fall into the *hot* category, but she found him appealing. He seemed quite shy and she liked that. For once she wasn't the shyest one in the room. When he glanced her way, she tried to convey all of what she was thinking in one smile, but she was afraid she probably looked more like a demented jack-o-lantern. To her surprise, Teddy smiled back. Butterflies began to roil in her tummy and her heart beat quickened uncomfortably. This would not be a good time for a panic attack. She took some long, slow deep breaths to calm this odd sensation she was feeling.

Mrs. MacDougall must have sensed the thickness of the air between the two. "This is so nice. I haven't had a Christmas gathering in years. Even though this one was impromptu, I think it's been a big success."

"I'll check to see if the snow has stopped. If it has, we should head back to the inn." Teddy went to the door and quickly returned. "'Tis still coming down quite heavily. I don't know how we'll get back."

"I've got an idea. Help me clean up and we'll see about getting the little one's back to their families."

CHAPTER 12

ALL IS WELL

A SHLEY AND CAILIN headed back to the inn. The others were still roaming up and down the street in search of gifts, but they had finished their shopping and Ashley was anxious to get back to Emma. The snow was piling up on the street and the sun had set early, as it did here during the Scottish winter months. Try as she might, Ashley couldn't help but worry about Emma. Cailin was always patient with her, understanding her concern and not making her feel badly about it.

They reached the inn door and she noted the lack of lights in the interior. "That's odd. There aren't any lights on. I hope everything's okay." The anxiety she felt whenever she thought Emma might be in danger came bubbling to the surface.

Cailin's arm was around her in a flash. "All is well, love. Ye'll see."

Entering the inn, she noted the quiet. You could hear a pin drop. Not something that was ever possible when the twins were around. "Cailin." Ashley glanced up at him and was not comforted to see that he wore a concerned expression now too.

"Teddy!" He called into what they both realized was an empty inn.

Ashley ran to the dining room, which was the last place they'd been seen and turned on the lights. There was not a sign of any of them. "Where could they be?"

"I dinnae ken. The snow is coming down in droves out there. Why would Teddy take them out in it?"

"Maybe they're upstairs. I'll go look," Ashley said.

"I'll check the cottage out back," Cailin responded.

Ashley bolted up the stairs, searching from room to room to no avail. When she arrived back downstairs, she was greeted by Cailin, who had a dark expression on his face. "They're not at the cottage?" she asked.

"Nae." Cailin paced back and forth for a moment. "Ashley, ye stay here. I'll go search for them."

"Don't you think we should let the others know first. That way Robert and Cormac can go with you to find them."

"Aye. I'll take care of it. Stay here in case they return."

He was out the door in a flash.

"We won't all fit in my tiny little car," Mrs. MacDougall was saying, "so I thought we might use this. Teddy, if ye'll help me please."

Teddy followed her and helped her remove a large canvas tarp from an old sleigh.

"I haven't used this in years, but it's large enough to fit everyone and 'twill be a fun way to get everyone safely back to the inn. Teddy, if ye'll help me move it to the center aisle of the stable, we can get Old Hildy hooked up to it and we'll be off. Marissa would ye mind folding the tarp for me."

Marissa went to work folding the tarp while Teddy helped move the sleigh. Once it was settled in the right spot according to Mrs. MacDougall, she pulled out a dust cloth and went over the interior making sure it was fit for occupants. Next she retrieved Old Hildy, who was a good-sized, chestnut draft horse with a sweet face. Teddy remembered her from those long ago Christmas holidays when a ride in Mrs. MacDougall's sleigh was the highlight of the festivities. Things had certainly changed over the years. He was older as was everyone else, including Mrs. MacDougall and Hildy. Glendaloch was lacking in small children, as most adults his age had moved to the larger cities for job opportunities, leaving behind a village stuck in time. Edna always said that he shouldn't worry, the others would return soon enough. Once they took the time to remember what a wonderful place it had been to grow up, they'd be back with their own children. Edna was always right. They'd be back and the little village would be lively once again no doubt.

The sleigh was ready to go and the children were seated comfortably with blankets to cover their legs. Marissa held the baby and Teddy held an umbrella, which he positioned in the best spot to block the snow from landing on Emma and Marissa. Mrs. Mac-Dougall clucked to Old Hildy and the sleigh began to move out into the late afternoon darkness and back to The Thistle & Hive.

THE CROWD GATHERED in front of the inn were shouting and throwing their hands in every direction. Edna had reassured them that the children were safe, but much to her dismay they hadn't really believed her. Even Maggie and Dylan were taking part in this crazy search and rescue mission.

"I'll head off towards the bridge," Cailin was saying. "Cormac ye head towards the stables. Robert and Ewan, ye can cover the other two directions." They all nodded their heads and were about to head off when the sound of sleigh bells caught their attention.

"Ye see, I told ye there was nae need to worry. Here they come now." Edna proclaimed.

All heads turned and watched as Mrs. MacDougall and her sleigh got closer and closer. Ashley, who was being comforted by Jenna, glanced up and with one last sniffle, broke away and started to run towards the sleigh, Cailin caught up with her and grabbing an arm, stopped her.

"They'll be here soon enough, love." He placed his arms around her to still her movement.

As the sleigh pulled up in front of the inn, the children were laughing and smiling at their parents, who all now wore relieved expressions.

"Edna, Merry Christmas to ye." Mrs. MacDougall sat atop the sleigh, reins in hand.

"And to ye, Frances. I see these little rascals made their way to yer stables." Edna helped Fiona get down from the sleigh. "Did ye have fun, Fiona?"

"Aye. We had cookies and hot chocolate."

"Did ye now?"

Wee Robert hopped off next. "Aye. We did. I wanted to check on Tonn, Da."

The parents were speechless. Caught between being angry that they'd gone off without permission and relief that they were safe. "There was nae need, Robbie. Mrs. MacDougall will see that they're cared for." Robert said. "Teddy, why would ye take them out in this weather?" Ashley had climbed up into the sleigh and grabbed Emma from Marissa.

Teddy was about to speak when Wee Robert spoke up. "Dinnae blame Teddy. 'Twas my fault. Teddy was tired and he fell asleep. I wanted to see Tonn, so we snuck away without him knowing."

"Ye shouldnae have gone without our permission. What if ye'd gotten lost? And ye should never have left here with wee Emma. Do ye ken?" Robert's stern tone was obviously getting his message across. Wee Robert nodded and gazed down at his feet. "There will be extra chores for ye to do when we return to Breaghacraig, lad."

"I'm sorry, Da. I shouldnae have done it." Wee Robert's voice began to quiver, but he stood tall and accepted his punishment like the little man he was. "I'm sorry Teddy." He turned first to Teddy and then to Ashley and Cailin. "I'm sorry I took Emma with me."

Cailin pulled him in for a hug. "All is well, ye'll ken better in the future. This is how we learn."

Teddy, who looked as if he'd like to melt into the nearest wall put a hand on Wee Robert's head. "'Tis alright, lad. I'll nae hold it against ye."

Edna knew Teddy well enough to know that he was still feeling responsible for what happened. "It's alright, Teddy. It could've happened to any one of us." She tut-tutted around the children, gathering them close and ushering them towards the door to the inn. "Mrs. MacDougall please come in and join us."

"I'm afraid I cannae. I must get back home. Marissa my dear, yer welcome to stay with me, if ye like."

Edna watched as Marissa and Teddy exchanged glances and she smiled to herself.

"I'd like that," Marissa said. "Bye Teddy. It was nice meeting you and the children."

Teddy gave a little half wave and the children all waved and shouted, "Bye."

Mrs. MacDougall turned the sleigh back towards the stables and as the others watched, she slowly disappeared into the falling snow.

THE CHILDREN HAD their dinner and then headed upstairs where Maggie and Dylan took turns reading them Christmas stories. The adults were eating later so they could relax and enjoy some wine and a good meal without the excited chatter of the little ones. Christmas Eve was the following day and they quietly reflected on their time here in Glendaloch.

Edna was on the phone with some last minute invitations and Angus was helping Dylan bring dinner to the table.

"Dylan, this looks amazing!" Angelina said. "I'm so proud of you. I didn't know you wanted to be a chef."

"Neither did I. It just sort of found me and I'm happy it did."

Bottles of wine were opened and everyone happily dug into their food. Hot homemade bread was passed, along with butter. The aroma was causing mouths to water.

Edna returned with a huge smile on her face. "We'll have some extra company with us tomorrow night." She glanced Teddy's way before continuing. "Frances and Marissa will be joining us." She was thrilled with Teddy's reaction, subtle though it was, she could see how happy it made him. "I also invited Dr. Ferguson." Lady Catherine's face lit up at this, although she too tried to hide her excitement.

"It's going to be a great celebration," Ashley said. Edna was happy she was more relaxed since seeing Dr. Ferguson.

"Edna ye and Angus have been a most gracious host and hostess. Thank ye so much for inviting us all." Robert raised his glass of wine. "I'd like to make a toast."

The others all picked up their glasses and waited to hear what Robert would say. ⊠To old friends and new. To family. To love. Sláinte!⊠

The others all replied in kind and then drank from their glasses.

Maggie leaned in to whisper to Dylan. "I think they like the food. It's so quiet." And since it was so quiet, everyone heard her and they all laughed and complimented Dylan on the delicious dinner.

CHAPTER 13

CHRISTMAS EVE

"GRANNY, CAN WE open our presents tonight?" Rowan pleaded. He'd been eyeing the pile of gifts under the tree ever since he'd arrived downstairs with his brother.

"Ye'll have to wait until tomorrow morning," Edna responded.

"Why Granny? Just one." He placed his hands palms together in a praying motion in front of his chest.

"Rowan, leave yer Granny alone." Ewan was inspecting all the packages set under the tree himself.

"Ma, perhaps we can do what we did when I was a little girl." Lena put a hand on each of her sons.

"Ye were a little girl, Ma?" Ranald asked.

"Yes, I was. What do ye think, Ma?" She looked to Edna, awaiting her answer.

"I think we can do that. Alright boys, if ye are good wee ones and ye eat all yer dinner, ye can open one gift tonight. Only one though, ye ken?"

"Us, too?" Wee Robert chimed in.

"Yes, all of ye."

The children jumped up and down their little faces filled with excitement.

"I believe ye've made them all verra, verra happy," Angus said.

"Aye. I'm a powerful one, I am." Edna laughed and then turning away from the tree addressed the adults. "Ye will have to wait until tomorrow morning, and I'll nay hear another word about it. Ewan, I'm talking to ye." Edna winked at Lena.

The door to the inn opened and Marissa and Frances walked in. Edna noted that Teddy sat up a little straighter in his seat when he saw them.

"Hi! Merry Christmas!" Marissa waved at everyone. "Hi, Teddy."

He waved back and gazed awkwardly in her direction. He was quite a shy one, but Edna thought if anyone could change that, it might be this adorable American lass.

The door opened again and this time Dr. Ferguson came in, followed by the Calhouns. "I'm so sorry I'm late. I got wrapped up in some paperwork and completely lost track of time."

"Yer not late, Arthur. Welcome Daniel and David. We were just about to sit down to eat. Come everyone, take yer seats."

Angus had put several of the dining room tables together to make one very long one. Maggie had decorated the table with festive greenery and ribbons. The Christmas themed dinnerware added to the holiday feeling, with red and green plaid napkins in the shape of Christmas trees, placed on each setting. Candles were lit all along the center of the table and plates of delicious food were set within easy reach of the guests.

DYLAN WAS PRETTY pleased with himself. He'd made many traditional Scottish dishes, including steak pie and roast goose. Vegetables were also in abundance, with many different ones to choose from to please everyone's taste. The guests happily passed platters of food down the table, with the parents, along with some help from the others, filling their children's plates before taking their own food. He smiled, happy that he had a hand in tonight's celebration. "How is it?" he asked Maggie as she took her first bite of the steak pie.

"Mmm…" she managed through a mouthful of food.

"Dylan, ye've done it again, lad. Delicious. We'll nae miss John when he leaves us." Angus had piled his plate high with all of his favorites.

"Thank you, Angus. It means a lot to me," Dylan replied.

"Aside from the fact that Dylan has made our Maggie so verra happy, we love having him here with us. He is a gem." Edna spoke to everyone at the table. "Shall we all raise our glasses to toast him?"

Everyone stopped what they were doing and picked up the glasses of champagne that had been set before them. The children had sparkling cider in their glasses and they felt very grown up being able to join in with the adults.

"A toast to a good man. A man who has made our lives much easier by his mere presence. And to a man who is a damn fine cook. To Dylan." Angus made the toast and then glasses were clinked all around as the others nodded in agreement.

Dylan felt good about his life here in Glendaloch. He felt loved and appreciated and he'd learned that he was so much more than the surfing football player he'd been back in San Francisco. He liked this much better. He'd found the love of his life and like his cousin Jenna and his friend Ashley, he'd found a family and in his mind, nothing could be better.

MAGGIE WAS so proud of Dylan. He'd gone above and beyond to make this Christmas Eve celebration special for everyone. The food was delicious, for which she was thankful. She wasn't much of a cook and had never truly been interested, so having a husband who cooked delicious meals every day was a dream come true.

"Maggie, how's Witchcraft 101 coming along," Jenna asked, using the term she'd heard Maggie call it in the past.

"You're a witch?" Marissa asked, a look of wonder on her face.

"Aye. So is me Auntie Edna." She smiled warmly at Marissa, who still appeared to be wrapping her brain around what she'd just heard. Maggie turned her attention back to Jenna. "Well, I think I'm in the advanced class now, wouldnae ye say, Auntie?"

"Aye. I think I've taught ye just about all that I ken. Ye no longer need me help. Yer a full-fledged witch, my dear." Edna beamed with pride.

"Coming from ye, that's high praise." Maggie's eyes twinkled with unshed tears of happiness. "I don't know if I'll ever get that meddling thing down that ye do so well."

"I'm a proud meddler, although I prefer to be called a matchmaker. The proof is right here at my dining table. My meddling… I mean my matchmaking has brought together most of the couples here tonight."

"I doubt that yer done though." Maggie glanced down the table at Teddy and Marissa who were engaged in a very animated conversation. "If ye ken my meaning."

"Aye. Verra observant of ye. I've more up me sleeve, but I'll nae speak of it now." Edna took a sip of her champagne. "Marissa, my dear. What brings ye to Glendaloch?"

Marissa looked up from her conversation with Teddy. "I'm here doing research for a book I'm writing."

"A book! How exciting! We've a famous author at our table." Edna raised her glass in Marissa's direction.

"Not famous at all, actually. This is my first book."

"What's it about?"

"Well, it's funny you should ask." Marissa hesitated for a moment before speaking again. "It's about a witch who helps people travel back in time."

Everyone stopped talking at once and glanced at each other.

"Did I say something wrong?"

"Nay. Of course not, dear. I'm sure ye'll laugh when I tell ye that everyone here has time travelled, with the exception of Teddy, Arthur, Frances and the Calhouns."

It was Marissa's turn to be silent. As a matter of fact, she looked like she might faint. Teddy grabbed hold of her hand, worry etching his brow.

"You're teasing me, aren't you?" Marissa sat up a bit taller and took a deep breath.

"Nae. I'm verra serious."

"I'm sorry. I'm having a hard time understanding. You mean to tell me that I came here to Scotland to research a time travel romance and I somehow stumbled upon two witches and a time travelling family."

"Aye." Edna knew it would take time for this to sink in, but she wasn't worried. She knew Marissa would eventually be more than fine with it.

"Is this true, Mrs. MacDougall?"

Frances had been eating her dinner and apparently doing her best not to get involved in this conversation. "Aye. I'm afraid so."

"Wow! I'm at a total loss for words and yet I have so many questions."

"Dinnae worry yerself. I'll answer any questions ye need answered and on the day after Christmas when everyone goes back to their own time, ye'll see how 'tis done. Maybe ye can put it in yer book."

"If you'll excuse me, I think I need some fresh air." Marissa stood, practically knocking her chair over in the process. Teddy steadied it and followed her as she headed outside, where the others watched as she paced back and forth in front of the window, with Teddy following along behind her.

"She'll be fine. 'Twas simply a shock to her system," Edna said. "Please, go back to yer meals. Children, dinnae shovel yer food into yer mouths. Take yer time. Ye'll have to wait until we're all done eating before ye can open yer gifts."

There was a collective grumble from the children as they pouted their disappointment.

"Dinnae fear, we'll be done eating in another hour or two," Edna teased.

"Granny!" Rowan exclaimed, causing the adults to burst into laughter.

"Rowan, my darling, we'll finish our dinner and then before we have dessert, we'll give ye each a gift to open. How does that sound?"

"I'm done," Ranald shouted.

Edna checked around the table. The children sat at attention, waiting. The adults were all smiling and nodding their heads. "Alright. Follow me and I'll give ye yer gift from Angus and I."

The children stood and ran to Edna who led them to the tree. She picked out two large boxes, almost as tall as Ranald and Rowan. "This is a gift for ye to share." The children appeared disappointed by this. "Ye'll see. 'Twill be far more fun when ye play with each other."

Rowan and Ranald tore into the wrapping paper, their little faces lit with anticipation. Wee Robert took charge of the MacKenzie children's package. When they'd finally gotten the paper off and had opened the box, they found hand carved castles populated by little tiny wooden people.

"'Tis beautiful," Fiona said. "Did ye make it?" She looked to Angus, who Edna noted stood proudly watching how happy he'd just made six little children.

"Aye. Do ye like it?" he asked.

"Aye. We love it." Wee Robert said.

"Angus you outdid yourself this time," Ashley said. "That is amazing."

"They'll have many happy years playing with it," Irene added. "Thank ye so verra much, Angus." She stood and went to him, throwing her arms around him and planting a kiss on his cheek.

The children were enthralled and played happily on the floor. The adults picked up their conversations where they'd been left off. Edna's gaze scanned the table and she knew it was time to exit to the kitchen. "I'll go get more champagne."

"I'll get it, Edna," Dylan volunteered.

"Nae. Ye sit and enjoy yerself. Ye've done enough this evening." She went through the kitchen doors, where she waited patiently. It wasn't long before the kitchen door opened and Cailin walked in.

"Edna, may I have a word with ye?" he asked.

"I was expecting ye, lad. What troubles ye? Although I believe I already ken the answer."

"'Tis Ashley. She wishes to stay here in Glendaloch."

"And ye dinnae wish to?"

"Nae, but I would stay for Ashley. I want her to be happy and I want her to stop worrying about Emma."

"I understand. Won't ye miss yer brother and sister?"

"Aye. I will." His head was bowed momentarily, but when he looked up at Edna she could see determination in his eyes. "Ashley is me wife and I love her more than life itself. I've been watching her suffer every day since Emma was born. She fears for our daughter's life and it causes her nothing but grief. I hate to see her this way. She has always been so happy. To see her smile was much the same as seeing the sun shining in the sky, but now it's as if she's always behind a very dark cloud. I cannae watch the pain she is in take her away from me. I'd do anything for her, even if it means I must leave me family."

"And ye need my help?" Edna was touched by his love and devotion to Ashley. She would help him in any way possible.

"We'll need a place to stay until we get settled here. Could we stay here with ye, in the cottage?"

"Of course. Ye are always welcome in my home. I love ye both as though ye were my own children."

"Thank ye, Edna. I'd ask that ye nae say a word. 'Twill be my gift to Ashley. I'll tell her tomorrow."

"As ye wish, Cailin."

He turned and left her alone in the kitchen, wondering what she could possibly do to help the situation. She had an idea. She only hoped it would work.

CHAPTER 14

CHRISTMAS DAY

I T WAS STILL dark when the children scurried downstairs, where Edna sat waiting for them, along with Angus who was thoroughly engrossed in his newspaper. The sun wouldn't rise for some time. Winter in the highlands meant extremely short days. The candlelight and warmth of the fireplace added a cheery ambience to what might otherwise be a depressing time of year. The fairy lights outside of the inn and up and down the street lent a magical quality to the little village of Glendaloch.

"Good morning, children!" Edna went to them, wrapping each one in a grandmotherly hug. "Why are ye up so early?" she teased.

The children rolled their eyes, something they'd learned from their time traveling aunties. Edna couldn't help but laugh. They were a delight and she cherished each and every moment she got to spend with them. It would break her heart to see them leave tomorrow, but she knew that she had the ability to arrange for visits, either in her time or theirs. It was something she planned to do more often now that she had help with the bridge.

"Do ye nae think ye should wait for yer parents?"

The children exchanged glances and then shook their heads vigorously.

Edna chuckled. "Well then, at least wait until I've served ye some hot chocolate. Come with me to the kitchen while we get everything we need."

The children gazed longingly back at the tree and gifts, but did as requested and followed Edna into the kitchen.

"Good morning," Ashley said as she yawned and stretched.

"Good morning." Jenna was seated on the sofa, coffee in hand. "I have such a hard time getting used to the fact that it's eight o'clock in the morning and still dark outside. You think I'd be used to it by now."

"I know." Ashley plopped herself down on the sofa next to Jenna.

"Is Emma still sleeping?" Jenna asked.

"She's all snuggled up with her daddy."

"I have to see this." Jenna rose and peeked into Ashley's room. "Awww… I wish I had a camera. That is the cutest thing I've ever seen."

Ashley always felt a pang of guilt when it came to Emma. Jenna wanted so badly to be a mother and was having a hard time. She understood how difficult it must be for her to see Cailin and Emma together. Jenna wanted that too and it simply wasn't happening. Ashley had reassured her that she should give it some time and not worry about it so much. She knew that Dr. Ferguson had told her the very same thing. The sad expression that was normally on Jenna's face as she observed Emma was gone this morning. It gave Ashley hope that Jenna was finally taking her advice.

"I'll bet the little ones are dying to open their gifts."

"We should probably get the guys up and head over to the inn. We don't want them to have to wait for us."

"True, but I was so enjoying the peace and quiet. Can we wait just a bit longer?"

The fire was blazing a bright warmth from the fireplace. Ashley nodded and sank into the sofa, finally at peace with herself and her future.

"WHERE IS EVERYONE?" Lena peered into the dining room. She could have sworn that she'd heard the children earlier, but they were nowhere to be seen. Worry clutched at her and she looked to Ewan for reassurance that they hadn't wandered off again.

"They're here somewhere. They wouldnae dare even think of going off without telling us," Ewan responded.

"Ye have much more faith in our boys than I do." Lena entered the room and headed straight for the kitchen, but before she could get there, the door opened and out marched the boys and their cousins. Each was carrying a tray of goodies, followed by Edna who had cups and a large urn, perched precariously on another, larger tray. Ewan jumped to her aid.

"Let me take that from ye, Mother."

EDNA DIDN'T HESITATE to turn her burden over to him. He set it on the sideboard near the fireplace. She loved that he called her mother. She couldn't have wished for anyone better for her only daughter.

"Children. Set yer trays down around the urn, please. Let's make them look as neat and pretty as possible." Edna supervised their efforts and was pleased to see Wee Robert and Fiona rearranging the decorations to create a festive setting. "Perfect."

"Robbie. Fiona. Go and wake yer ma and da. Tell them to hurry down, we're waiting for them."

The two ran up the stairs and could be heard knocking loudly on their parent's door.

"What is it?" Irene's startled voice carried down the stairs.

"Auntie Edna says 'tis time to get up."

"Tell her we'll be right there."

The children ran back downstairs with the message and it was only moments later when Irene and Robert made their entrance much to the delight of the waiting children's.

"Shall we go get Uncle Cailin and Uncle Cormac?" Fiona asked.

"No need. I believe they'll be here any moment." Edna smiled as the door opened and they all walked in "See? I told ye."

Richard, and his family were next to appear, followed by Maggie, Dylan and Chester.

The adults went for the food and the children headed straight to the tree. Edna and Angus began handing out gifts to each of them, as the adults nibbled on pastry and watched the glee with which the children opened their gifts. Each present had been chosen to suit the time and place it would be returning to with the children and based on their reactions, the children were quite pleased with their treasures. They each also received a Christmas stocking filled with fruits and chocolate and some smaller keepsakes.

The sound of sleigh bells could be heard approaching the inn and a few moments later, the door opened. Arthur Ferguson held the door for Frances and Marissa to enter.

"Merry Christmas," Dr. Ferguson said as he closed the door. He had a large basket covered with a red towel, which Frances took from him and handed to Edna.

"Marissa and I did some baking last night. It's our gift to ye."

"Thank ye, Frances. How thoughtful."

"Yer the thoughtful one, inviting us all here to enjoy Christmas day with ye and yer guests."

Edna put the basket down and pulled Frances in for a hug. "We've been friends for many years. I'm sorry it's taken me this long to invite ye to join us."

"Nae worries, my dear. Before this I always had me husband and children to spend the day with."

Edna noted a slight change in her eyes. Frances was not one to wear her heart on her sleeve, preferring to always show a happy face, so as not to have others feeling badly for her. Her husband had passed away only last year and her children were off on their own adventures. Edna had no doubt they'd be back some day, but until then Frances spent more time with the animals she cared for than with the people of Glendaloch. That was going to have to change and Edna would make it her mission to see to it.

As for Marissa, she'd come prepared with a notebook today and had already begun asking questions of the MacKenzies. She busily jotted down the information she was receiving, while at the same time scanning the room.

"He'll be here shortly. He's helping out by picking up some last minute gifts." Edna assumed she was searching for Teddy and she was right.

"Oh. I was wondering where Teddy was. I didn't know if he had somewhere else to be today."

"Only here with us, dear. He'll be happy to see ye've joined us."

"Do you really think so?"

"I do. Come sit with me for a moment. I'll be happy to answer any questions ye may have about time travel, or being a witch."

TEDDY SNUCK IN through the kitchen door of the inn, carefully setting the baskets he carried on the floor. He tucked one special gift into his jacket pocket before entering the dining room of the inn.

"Teddy, there ye are. We've been waiting for ye," Edna said.

He nodded to Edna, all the while thinking to himself that he needed to start speaking more. He'd felt so comfortable last night with Marissa. She understood him and had encouraged him to come out of his shell. All his life he'd felt like the odd man out. Being different hadn't been easy and growing up in this little village had been difficult. There were times when the other lads of the village had taken great pleasure in making his life as miserable as possible. If it wasn't for Edna, he wasn't sure where he'd be today or if he even would be for that matter.

He loved the way Marissa's face lit up when she saw him. He'd never experienced anything like that in his entire life. "Merry

Christmas!" he said, straightening to his full height and attempting eye contact with everyone. It felt good. They all smiled and wished him the same. That wasn't so hard. Marissa was beaming at him and he beamed right back. He pulled that neatly wrapped package from his pocket and walked to her. "This is for ye."

"Really? For me?" She accepted the package from him and stared down at it. "I don't have anything for you."

"Ye've already given me my gift. Ye encouraged me to speak and be heard. I intend to do that from now on. Thank ye for that."

"You're welcome." She gently untied the ribbon and ran her finger under the tape. The package fell open, revealing a beautiful hand tooled purple leather notebook accompanied by a matching pen."

"Because yer a writer," Teddy said.

Marissa jumped up and threw her arms around him. It took only a moment for Teddy's arms to find their way around Marissa. He was holding her close and not feeling at all awkward. What a relief. She felt good in his arms. He could definitely get used to this.

"Thank you, Teddy. It's the most beautiful gift anyone has ever given me and so thoughtful." She kissed his cheek and moved back out of his arms. Teddy's hand automatically went to his cheek, where he could still feel the softness of her lips as they'd left an indelible impression on him. He'd remember it forever.

"I ken ye'll be leaving soon, and I wanted to give ye something to remember me by." His voice took on a solemn note.

"Oh, Teddy. I guess I do have a gift for you after all. Mrs. Mac-Dougall has extended an invitation to stay with her as long as I like. I'll help her around the house and stable and I'll be able to write my book."

Teddy was so happy that he swept Marissa up in his arms and twirled her around, completely oblivious to everyone present in the room. When he finally put her down he glanced at Edna and the others who were all smiling brightly at them.

"That's wonderful news, Marissa," Edna replied with a sparkle in her eyes.

Teddy knew that sparkle. He'd seen it many times before. He never thought he'd see it directed at him, but there it was, plain as day. Edna had been matchmaking again and he was very thankful that she had.

JENNA EXCUSED HERSELF and headed to the kitchen. She was being followed by Cormac.

"Where do ye think yer going, love?" Cormac blocked her way into the kitchen.

"I'm going in the kitchen. What does it look like I'm doing?"

"What do ye need. I'll be happy to retrieve it for ye."

"I can get it myself. Thanks though." She tried breezing past him, only to find an arm in her way. "Cormac, please. There's something in the kitchen I have to get."

"What is it?"

"Why are you behaving like this." When he didn't answer her or move, she said, "Okay. Your present is in there."

"What?" Cormac appeared puzzled. "Yer gift is in there." He pushed open the door and Jenna practically knocked him over to get in first.

They both stopped short when they saw two baskets with red ribbons attached. "Which one is which?" Jenna asked.

"Teddy!" Cormac called. "Why are there two baskets?"

"Ye each asked me to pick something up for ye this morning and I did." Teddy peeked his head through the door. "The one on the right is the one Jenna asked me to get and the one on the left is yers, Cormac."

The puzzled couple exchanged suspicious glances and then each grabbed their gift basket. "Let's go back in the other room," Cormac suggested.

"Okay."

Cormac held the door open for Jenna and then followed her back to their seats.

"Merry Christmas, my love," Cormac handed his basket to her.

"Merry Christmas, Cormac." Jenna smiled sweetly at him as she handed his gift to him. "Open yours first."

Cormac lifted the cloth covering and a small version of Chester poked his head out. "Jenna…" He gazed at her with a questioning expression. "Why…"

"I know how much you want to be a father and I know it will happen at some point. I also know how much you love Chester and how much you've missed him since he left with Dylan, so I thought this little puppy might be just what you need right now." He lifted the pup from the basket and brought it up to touch noses with the little creature.

"Thank ye, 'tis a wonderful surprise and one I'm so verra happy to receive." He had a funny grin on his face as he said, "Now open yers."

Jenna did as instructed and gasped when she too pulled out a tiny puppy. "Oh, Cormac, it's adorable."

"I've been told she'll be a tiny dog. Perfect fer ye to carry with ye wherever ye go. My reasons are much the same as yers, my lady love."

Tears brimmed in Jenna's eyes as she leaned her head on his shoulder, both pups now snuggled in their arms.

"This doesnae mean we'll stop trying to have a bairn," Cormac teased.

"I hope not," Jenna replied. "That's the best part."

EVERYONE HAD EXCHANGED their gifts. Robert received instructions on how to make a much more practical camping shower, which pleased him to no end. He gave Irene a kit filled with embroidery floss and needles. She loved to do needlework, so it was a perfect gift for her and she marveled at all the colors he'd chosen.

Richard and Angelina didn't buy individual gifts, but instead purchased something they'd share. They chose two beautiful wine goblets nestled in a velvet lined box. Catherine received a beautiful cashmere shawl, which she immediately wrapped herself in.

Ewan and Lena also shared a gift, a beautifully crafted backgammon game to play in front of the fire at night.

"What about you?" Ashley asked Edna.

"Never fear. I've her gift right here." Angus handed a large envelope to Edna, who looked quite surprised.

"I've nothing for ye, Angus. I've been so busy with our guests that I didn't even think about us."

"Never ye mind, love. Open it. 'Twill be a gift for me as well."

Edna opened the envelope and gasped. Inside were travel brochures for Costa Brava in Spain, along with plane tickets. "Oh, Angus. This is so wonderful. I've always wanted to go to Spain. But, who'll…"

"Don't worry, Auntie. As our gift to ye, Dylan and I will be taking care of everything back here in Glendaloch. Leave everything to us and ye go and relax. Ye deserve the time away." Maggie and Dylan hugged Edna, who was sniffling and getting teary-eyed.

"Yer all too good to me," she managed to squeak out.

"Everyone in this room knows that you're the one who's been good to us," Dylan said.

"Edna, that's so exciting!" Frances said. "Ye'll have a verra good time. I went once, many years ago and I'll never forget it."

"Thank ye, Angus. And thank ye Maggie and Dylan. I didn't mean to get all weepy on ye, but this was quite the surprise." She wiped her eyes with her hankie. "But what about ye two? Where are yer gifts?" Edna said to Maggie.

"We've decided that when ye get back from yer trip, we're going to take a little break as well. We haven't decided where we're going yet."

"We've got lots of places in mind, now we just need to settle on one." Dylan gazed at Maggie, who nodded her agreement.

"Is that everyone? Have we all exchanged our gifts?" Edna asked.

"Not yet. I've got something for my husband," Ashley said. She went to the tree and removed a small box, which she brought to Cailin. "For you, sweetie. I hope you like it."

Cailin accepted the gift with one hand and took Ashley's hand with the other. "What could it be?"

"You have to open it to see," Ashley said.

Carefully unwrapping the package, Cailin took his time, apparently knowing that it would drive Ashley crazy. She was squirming in anticipation. He finally opened the box and pulled out a pair of blue baby booties. His eyes went immediately to Ashley and he stood, pulling her into his chest and practically crushing her in his embrace. It was obvious that he couldn't speak.

"I guess Jenna did a very good job of keeping my secret," she said, pulling herself free and gasping for breath. Ashley glanced around at all the happily surprised faces in the room.

"Ashley." Cailin cleared his throat. "I've been doing a lot of thinking since we've been here in Glendaloch and I want ye to live a life that is happy and free of worry, so my gift to ye is one I know ye've been wanting. I've spoken with Edna, and our little family will be staying here in Glendaloch when everyone leaves tomorrow.

It was Ashley's turn to be silent.

Irene, on the other hand, gasped at the announcement. "Cailin, ye cannae. I'll miss ye so." She burst into tears, which triggered tears from all of his little nieces and nephews.

"No, uncle, dinnae leave us." Wee Robert said, running to Cailin and doing his best to wrap his arms around him.

"I'll come back to visit as often as I can," Cailin assured him. "'Tis important to Ashley to stay here and as her husband, I cannae deny her heart's desire."

The whole room fell silent. This was what Ashley wanted, but somehow now that she'd gotten her wish, she found she wasn't as happy about it as she should be. She realized that watching her family leave tomorrow would not make her happy at all. She didn't know what to do or what to say. Glancing around the room, her eyes locked on Edna. "Edna?"

"Yes, dear. Is something wrong? Don't ye wish to stay here?"

"I thought I did. Now I'm not so sure." Ashley turned to Cailin, who seemed sadder than she'd ever seen him.

"Ashley, what are ye saying?"

"I don't know. I don't know what to do."

"I've a thought," Edna said. "Why do ye nae take the rest of today and tonight to think about it. No need to decide right this moment. Ye can tell us in the morning, aye?"

"Okay. I guess." Ashley felt terrible about this. She was ruining everyone's day. They should all be enjoying their last day here, but instead they all looked as if someone had died. She felt the weight of the world on her shoulders, knowing that her decision could separate her and Cailin from the family she'd come to love so very much.

CHAPTER 15

ECEMBER 26TH HAD come far too quickly for Edna's liking. She'd enjoyed having everyone here with her and hated to see them go. Dylan prepared a lovely breakfast for them, and knowing they had a long trip ahead, he'd also packed plenty of food for them to take along as they headed home to the year 1516.

"I wonder what Ashley will decide?" Angus asked. He was concerned about the family being split apart. "They are such a close knit group, leaving Cailin and Ashley behind will be like severing a limb for them."

"Before they go, I'm going to speak with Ashley. I have some news that may help her with her decision. If ye'll excuse me, I'm going back to the cottage to speak with her."

Angus' face and smile told Edna he knew what she might be up to. "Good luck."

"Thank ye, me love, but I won't need it."

Edna went out through the kitchen door and garden, heading for the cottage. Upon reaching it, she knocked on the door, to be greeted by Jenna and Cormac, who had packed all their things and were obviously heading for the inn, where they'd meet the rest of their group of time travelers.

"Good morning, Edna." Jenna said. "Thank you again for taking such good care of us."

"Aye." Cormac added. "We love ye, Edna."

"Thank ye. The feeling is mutual. I'll see ye in the dining room. Dylan has set out a lovely breakfast for all of ye."

"I think you're needed in there," Jenna said as she headed for the inn.

Edna walked in to find Ashley in tears and Cailin doing his best to console her. "Cailin, would ye mind if I spoke with Ashley alone for a moment."

"Of course." Cailin kissed the top of Ashley's head and went into the bedroom, closing the door behind him.

Ashley broke into a whole new round of crying as Edna sat next to her and cradled her in her arms. "I'm destroying the family that I wanted to badly. What is wrong with me?"

"Well, if I had to guess, I'd say ye were probably going through a bout of postpartum anxiety. Dr. Ferguson agrees with me."

"What can I do about it? I'm so exhausted from worrying all the time."

"I ken ye are. Do ye remember before ye met Cailin? Do ye remember that ye suffered from anxiety and had for years?"

"When I met Cailin that all went away."

"It did, but having a baby that ye love so much, has caused it to rear its ugly head once again. The thing that ye've forgotten is that yer husband is there to help ye. He'd slay any monster for ye if he could and he'd lay down his life for yer bairns. The anxiety monster is a bit more difficult. Cailin can't see it to fight it." Edna checked Ashley to see if she understood. "Ye see, Ashley, no matter where ye live, whether 'tis here, Breaghacraig or San Francisco, yer going to have these difficulties. The difference is that at Breaghacraig, ye have an army of people who love ye. They want to help ye."

"I know they do."

"Then let them. Let Irene have Emma for a few hours or Jenna perhaps. Take some time for yerself. Get outside of yer head and enjoy the little things in life. Ye've a fine braw husband. Enjoy him."

"So you think I should go back."

"'Tis not up to me, dear. Ye've got to make that decision."

"But what if Emma gets sick? What will I do?" Ashley started to get choked up again.

"Well, that hasnae happened yet. Why worry about it before ye have to? Besides, I've had a talk with Dr. Ferguson and he's agreed to be available for ye whenever ye need him."

"He'd do that?"

"Why yes, he would. He would like to see Lady Catherine again and in order to do that, he'll need to travel back in time. He may even stay, ye never know."

"But you do." Ashley said, brushing the tears from her eyes and grabbing a tissue for her nose.

Edna laughed. She did know, but things would unfold in their own time, with only the slightest prodding from her. "Ye ken, ye still have yer magick backpack."

"I do."

"Well, I'm going to give ye one more item to add to it." Edna reached into her jacket pocket, pulling out a snow globe and handing it to Ashley.

"Is that The Thistle & Hive inside?"

"It is. Clever wouldnae ye say?" Edna chuckled. "If ye ever need to get in touch with me, or if ye need Dr. Ferguson, all ye need do is call to me while yer holding this. Go ahead, try it and see."

"But you're right here."

"I ken that, but I want ye to see how it works."

Ashley lifted the snow globe and looked into it. "Edna, are ye there?" Much to Ashley's surprise, Edna's face appeared in the globe. She looked up and Edna smiled warmly at her.

"Ye see, there I am."

"Amazing!"

"Now, ye will have to share it with the others, so be sure to let them know how it works and keep it somewhere they can get to it if need be."

"It sounds like you think I've already made up my mind."

"Have ye?"

"Yes. I'm going back."

"I'll leave ye to tell yer husband. Then get yer things together and come over to the inn for some breakfast."

"Thank you, Edna. You're truly my faerie godmother."

"Thank ye, darlin', but I'm nae faerie. I'll be yer witchy godmother." Chuckling to herself, she left the cottage.

EDNA, ANGUS AND the others were all seated in the dining room enjoying Dylan's hard work, when Ashley and Cailin entered. Emma was wrapped in her sling and attached to Cailin's chest.

"What's this?" Irene asked. "Are ye coming back with us?"

"Aye, sister. We are." Cailin was absolutely gleeful. He would have stayed if Ashley had wanted, but he was relieved when she told him she wanted to go home.

"Thank ye, Edna. I ken this was yer doing."

"I'm going to need all of your help," Ashley announced. "I can't do this alone. I'm going to need babysitters."

"What is a babysitter?" Irene appeared puzzled.

"Someone who watches your baby for you while you go do something else," Ashley explained.

"I'd be happy to do that for ye," Irene stated.

"We all would," Jenna added.

"And Dr. Ferguson will come and visit us, too." Ashley blurted.

Cailin noted that Lady Catherine's ears perked up at the mention of Dr. Ferguson.

"He'll be here soon to say goodbye to ye all," Edna said.

Cormac and Jenna each had their new little pups in their arms. Chester was curious to see them and sat at attention in front of Cormac. "Dinnae worry Chester, ye'll always hold a special place in me heart, as I ken I do in yers." He bent down to scratch Chester behind the ears and at the same time let him sniff the puppy. "Now even though I'll miss ye, this little one will be with me." Chester cocked his head to the side and everyone laughed. "Why do ye laugh? He understands what I'm saying to him."

"I don't doubt that he does," Dylan added. "He's pretty intuitive."

"Shall we go get the horses," Angus asked.

"Aye." Robert said.

The men, along with Wee Robert, all headed off down the street to the stable, where they would gather their horses and return for the women.

They were no sooner out the door when Dr. Ferguson arrived. "I came to say my goodbyes. I saw the men heading off down the street as I arrived."

"They'll be back shortly," Edna said. "Would anyone like to help me in the kitchen. I'm going to check in with Dylan to see if he needs any help."

"I'll go with you," Angelina said.

"Me, too." Lena added

Jenna and Ashley got the hint and followed Edna, leaving Lady Catherine alone with Dr. Ferguson.

"Catherine, I wanted to speak with ye before ye left."

"I'm happy that ye did, Arthur."

He took Catherine's hand and led her to a settee in the lobby. "Please, sit." He cleared his throat. "Catherine, I'll be visiting yer time soon and I was wondering if ye'd allow me to call on ye."

"I'd be delighted, Arthur. As a matter of fact, my feelings may be hurt if ye didn't."

Arthur relaxed. He'd felt something for Catherine the moment she walked into his office. At first he thought the fact that she lived in another time would be a huge deterrent to any relationship with her, but then Edna had approached him with a plan to help Ashley to overcome her anxiety and he'd been more than happy to agree.

"Yer a fascinating woman, Catherine and I'd like to get to

know ye better."

"I'd like that, Arthur. I'd like that very much."

"Good. Then I'll plan to see ye in the next month or so. Ye've made me a verra happy man." Arthur thought that as an older gentleman, his chance at finding love was nonexistent, but maybe not. Maybe he could find a way to make this strange arrangement work. And if he couldn't figure it out, he knew Edna well enough to know that she would.

He was still holding Catherine's hand and he intended to keep holding it until she left. He had no idea whether that was appropriate in her time and he really didn't care. Besides, it didn't appear that she was interested in letting go either.

WHEN THE MEN finally returned, they brought Teddy and Marissa with them. He'd been at the stable visiting with her and they wanted to come back to the inn to say their goodbyes properly.

"Is everyone ready?" Robert asked as he dismounted.

The rest of the men followed suit and the goodbyes began in earnest. Everyone wanted to hug Edna, Angus, Maggie and Dylan. Teddy and Marissa joined in, hugging everyone and saying that they hoped to see them again soon. Marissa mentioned that she'd like to experience time travel as research for her book.

The flurry of activity came to a sudden stop as everyone realized that they'd said all of their goodbyes. They'd kissed everyone and hugged everyone. There was nothing left to do but mount their horses and head for the bridge.

Edna and those remaining in Glendaloch followed along on the path. Edna, of course, to make sure everything went as it was supposed to. Marissa wanted to see how it worked with her own eyes and the others just wanted to wave to their friends one last time as they disappeared from sight.

As they approached the bridge, the horses became a bit nervous, snorting and prancing in place. They were leaving with considerably more than they'd arrived with, but they'd packed everything and distributed it evenly among all the horses. They waited in silence for the fog to come and as they waited, Robert spoke. "Edna and Angus, we wanted to get ye a gift to thank ye for all ye've done for us, but we couldnae find a thing that would suffice. So, with a little help and magick from Maggie we found a way to send ye images of all of us from time to time. Ye'll be able to watch yer grandsons grow. We'll send them from every occasion. 'Twill be as if yer with us."

"Aye, Auntie. I've created a magic picture frame for each family. All they need do is stand in front of it and utter a simple spell. It will automatically transmit the photo back here to ye through a picture frame here on our end."

Edna was speechless. Tears welled in her eyes again and Angus laid a comforting hand on her shoulder. "I don't know what to say. Ye are all my family and knowing that ye are well and happy is my only wish."

"We'd also like to extend an invitation for ye to come and stay with us anytime ye'd like."

"That would be wonderful, Robert. Thank ye. I will definitely take ye up on that offer."

The first wisps of fog floated across the bridge and became thicker and thicker until they covered everything. Robert turned and waved, as did the others.

"Beira will be waiting for ye on the other side." Edna couldn't help herself, tears continued streaming down her cheeks. Ashley blew her a kiss and Edna noted that she too had red rimmed eyes. And then before she knew it, they had all ventured into the fog and the colorful little pops of light flashed throughout, telling her that they were on their way. A few moments passed and the fog lifted, leaving an empty clearing on the other side of the bridge. They were gone.

"Shall we?" Angus placed a soothing arm around Edna's shoulders and turned her away from the bridge. The others followed as they headed back to the inn, where life would get back to normal once more, or at least as normal as it could get with Edna around.

ACKNOWLEDGMENTS

I'D LIKE TO thank my editor Jen Graybeal for her help getting this novella ready for publishing. Thank you to my cover artist, Sheri McGathy of Cover Art by Sheri for bringing Edna Campbell to life on this cover.

ABOUT THE AUTHOR

JENNAE VALE IS a best selling author of romance with a touch of magic. As a history buff from an early age, Jennae often found herself day-dreaming in history class - wondering what it would be like to live in the places and time periods she was learning about. Writing time travel romance has given her an opportunity to take those daydreams and turn them into stories to share with readers everywhere.

Originally from the Boston area, Jennae now lives in the San Francisco Bay area, where some of her characters also reside. When Jennae isn't writing, she enjoyed spending time with her family and her pets, and daydreaming, of course.

CONNECT WITH JENNAE

Twitter.com/jealil
Facebook.com/JennaeValeAuthor

www.jennaevaleauthor.com
jennaevaleauthor@gmail.com

www.ingramcontent.com/pod-product-compliance
Lightning Source LLC
Chambersburg PA
CBHW070634130626
46555CB00006B/2546